Pokémon™ Legendary and Mythical Coloring Adventures

SCHOLASTIC INC.

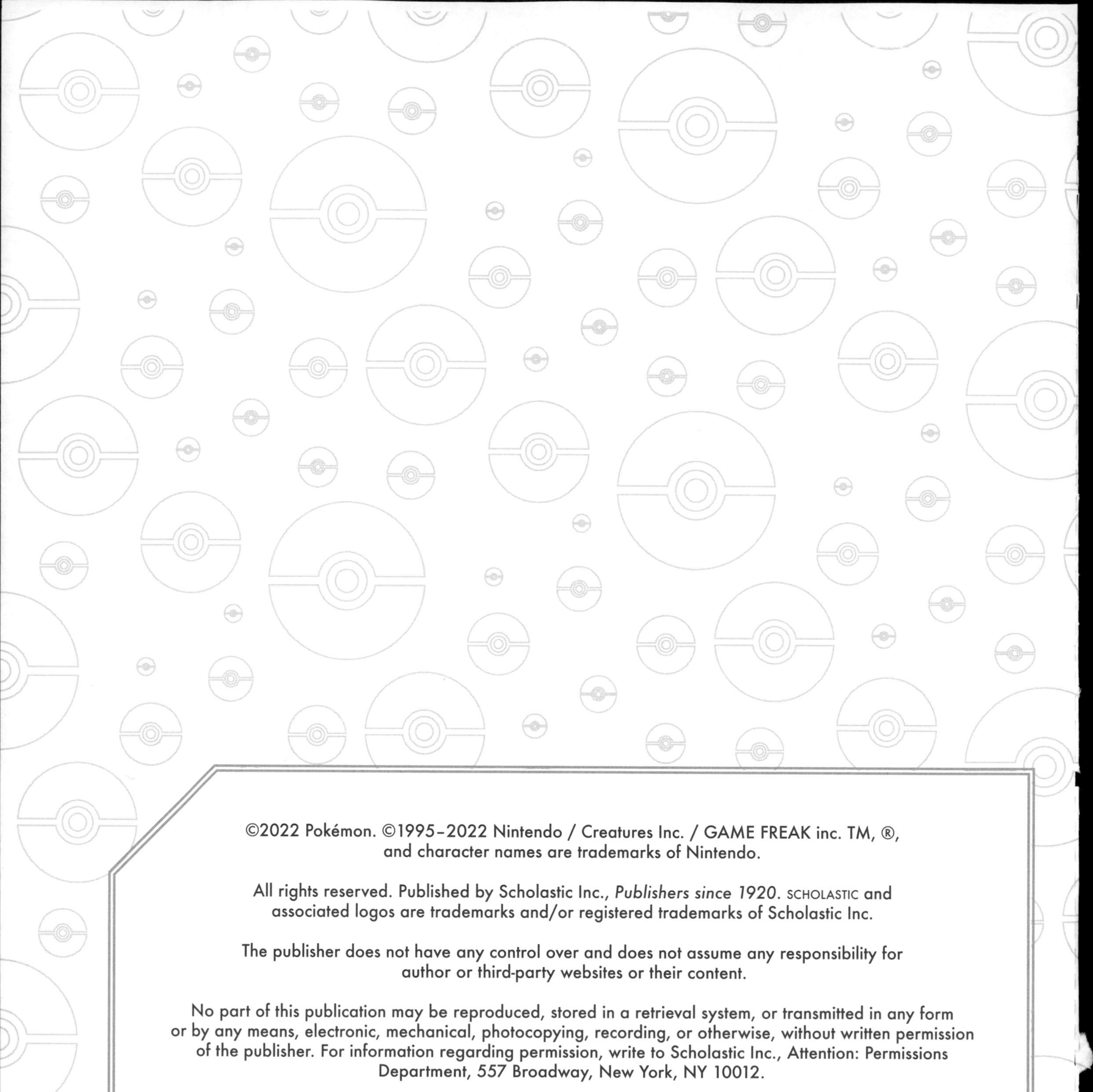

ISBN 978-1-338-81996-0

10 9 8 7 6 5 4 3 22 23 24 25 26

Printed in the U.S.A. 40
First printing 2022
Designed by Becky James

LUGIA

MEWTWO

MEGA MEWTWO X
MEGA MEWTWO Y

LATIOS
LATIAS

MEGA LATIOS
MEGA LATIAS

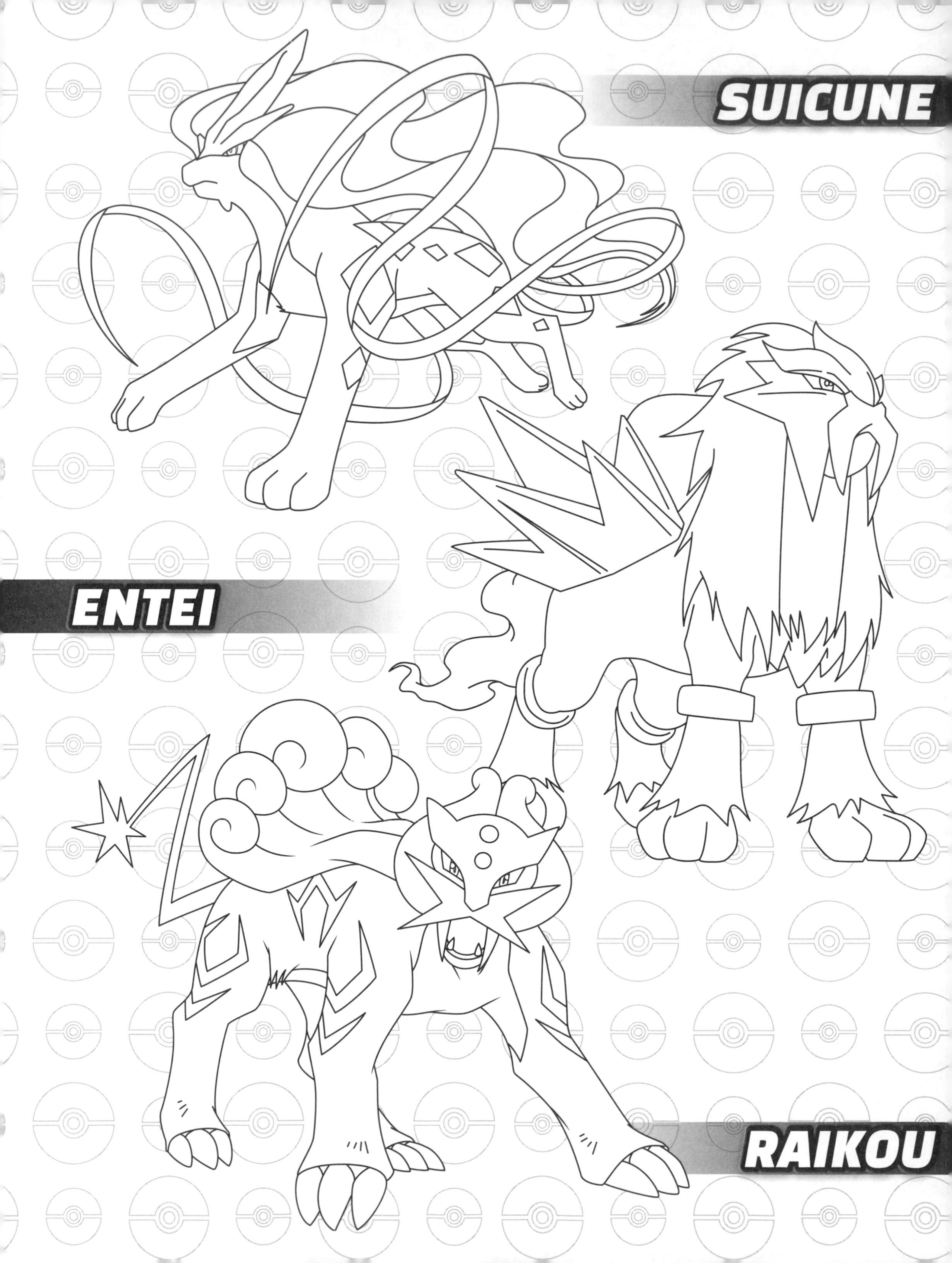
SUICUNE
ENTEI
RAIKOU

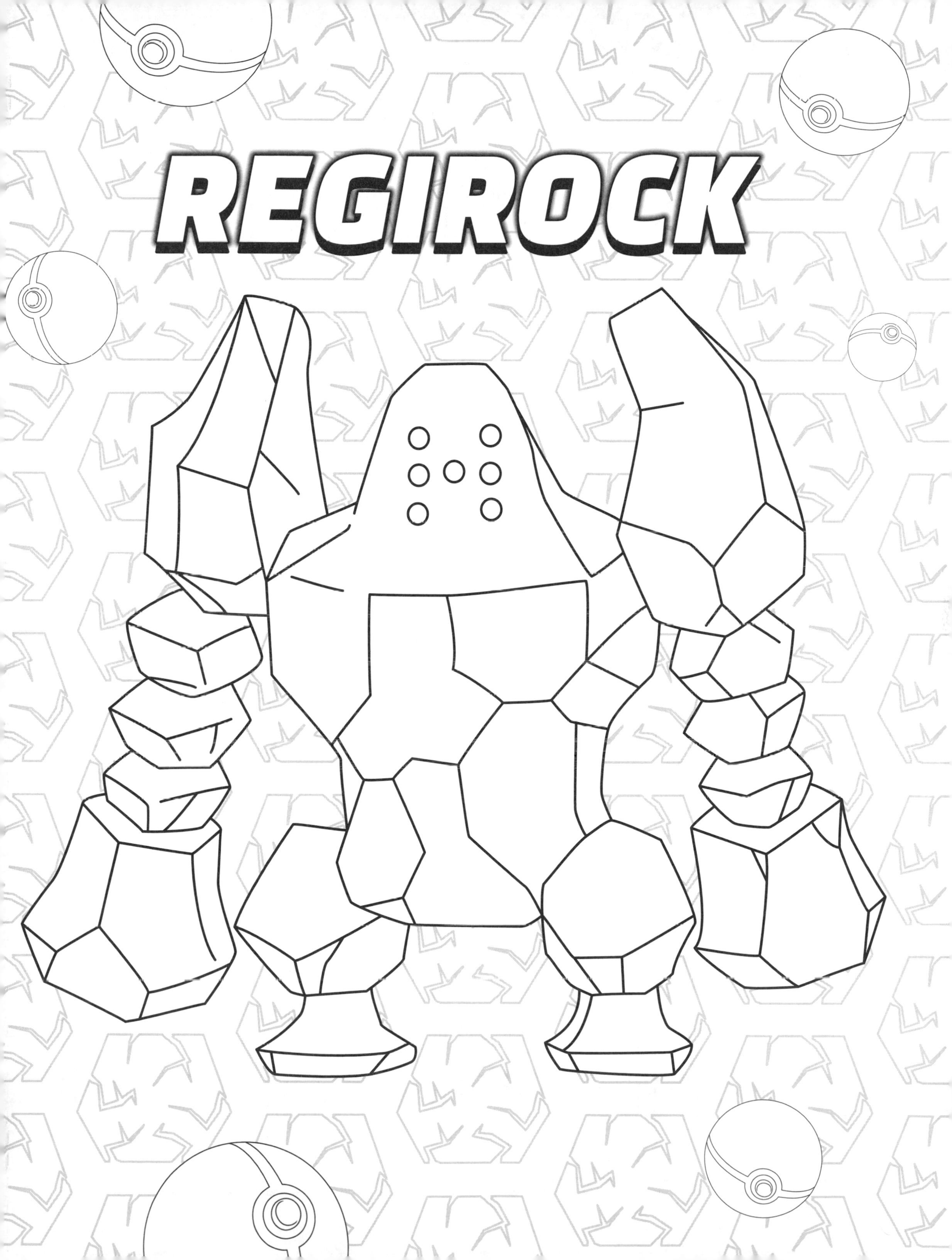
REGIROCK

MELTAN

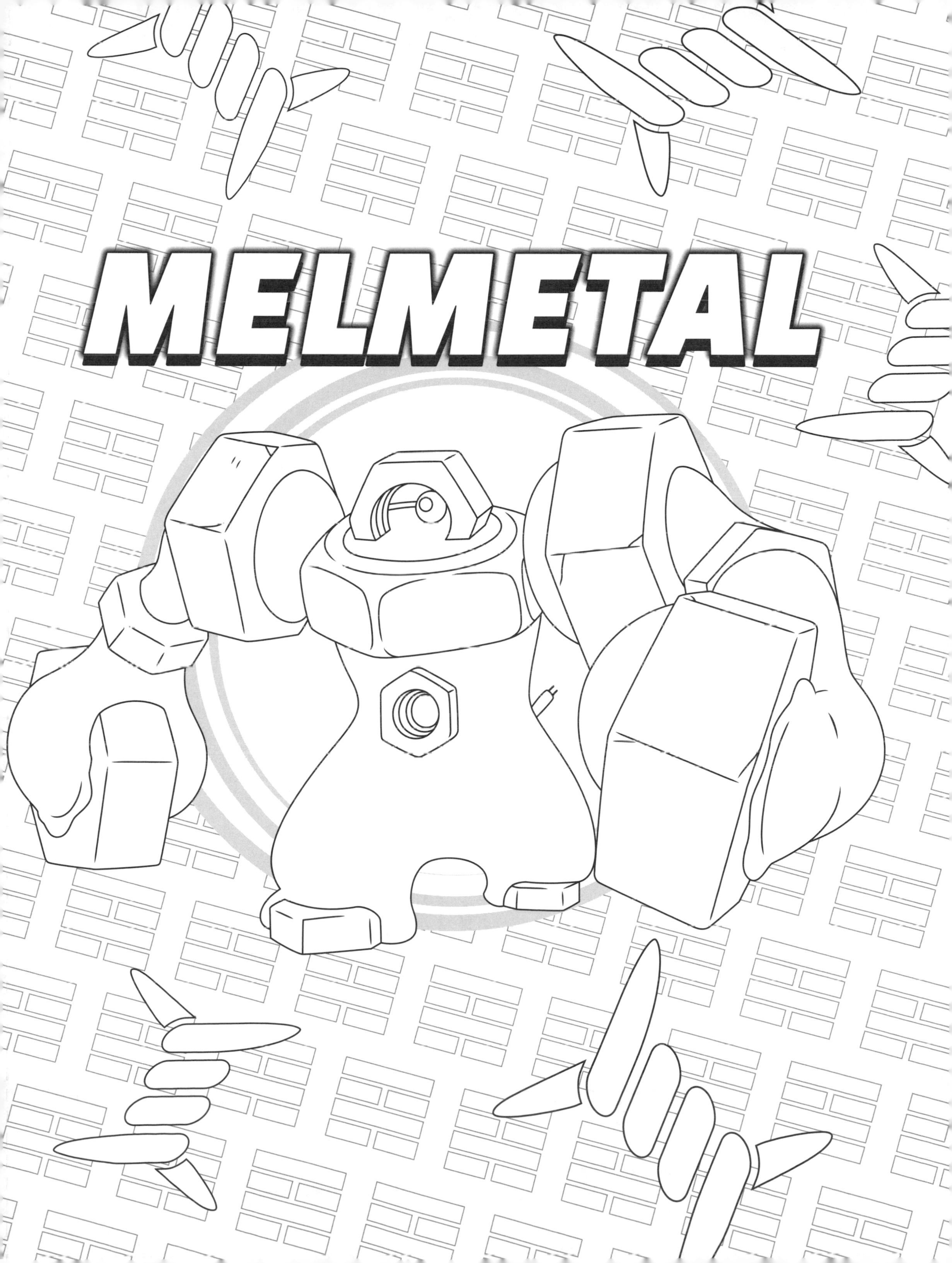
MELMETAL

HO-OH

KYUREM

WHITE KYUREM

BLACK KYUREM

REGICE

COBALION
TERRAKION
VIRIZION

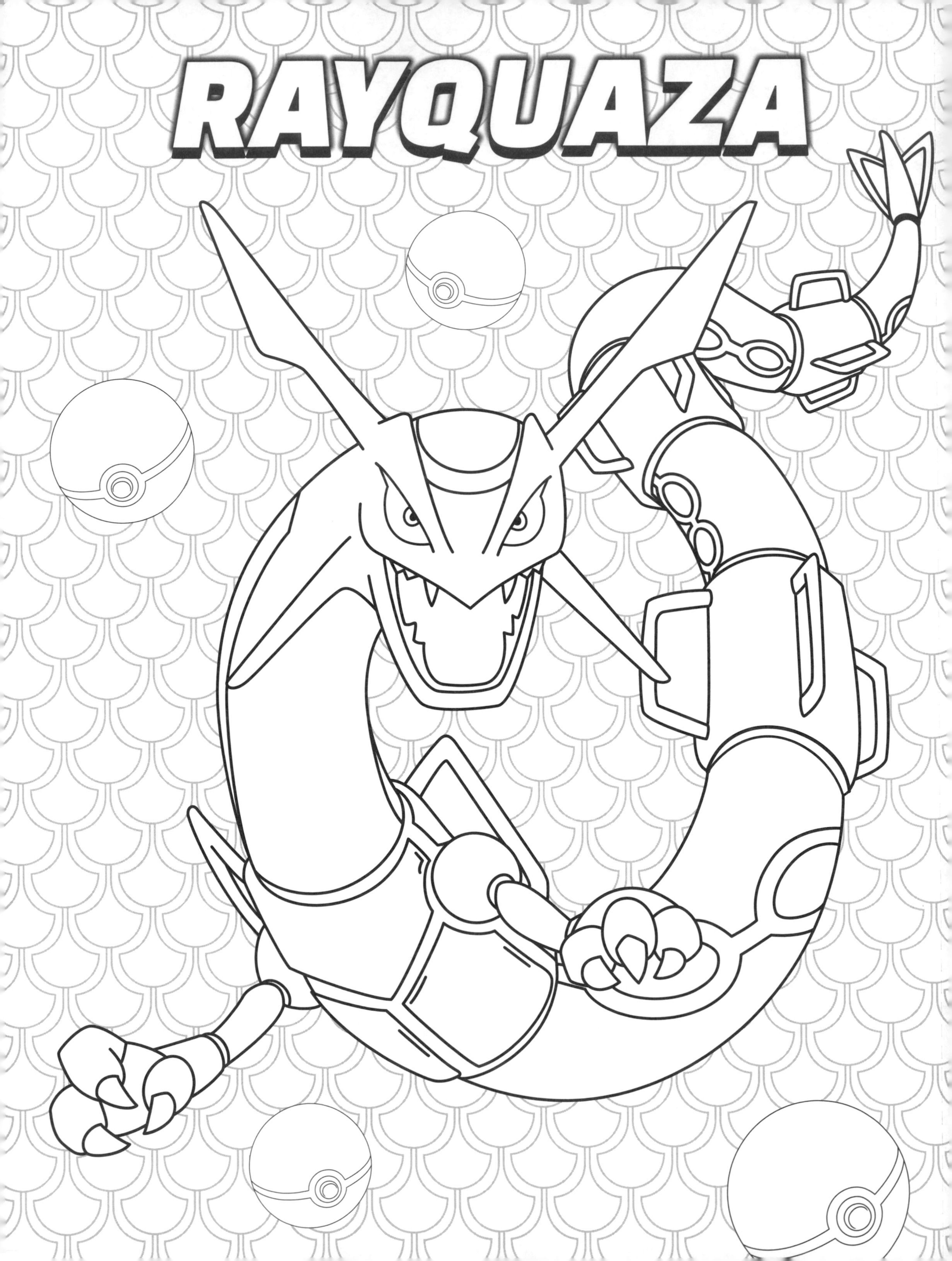
RAYQUAZA

MEGA RAYQUAZA

DEOXYS

NORMAL FORME

ATTACK FORME

SPEED FORME

DEFENSE FORME

JIRACHI

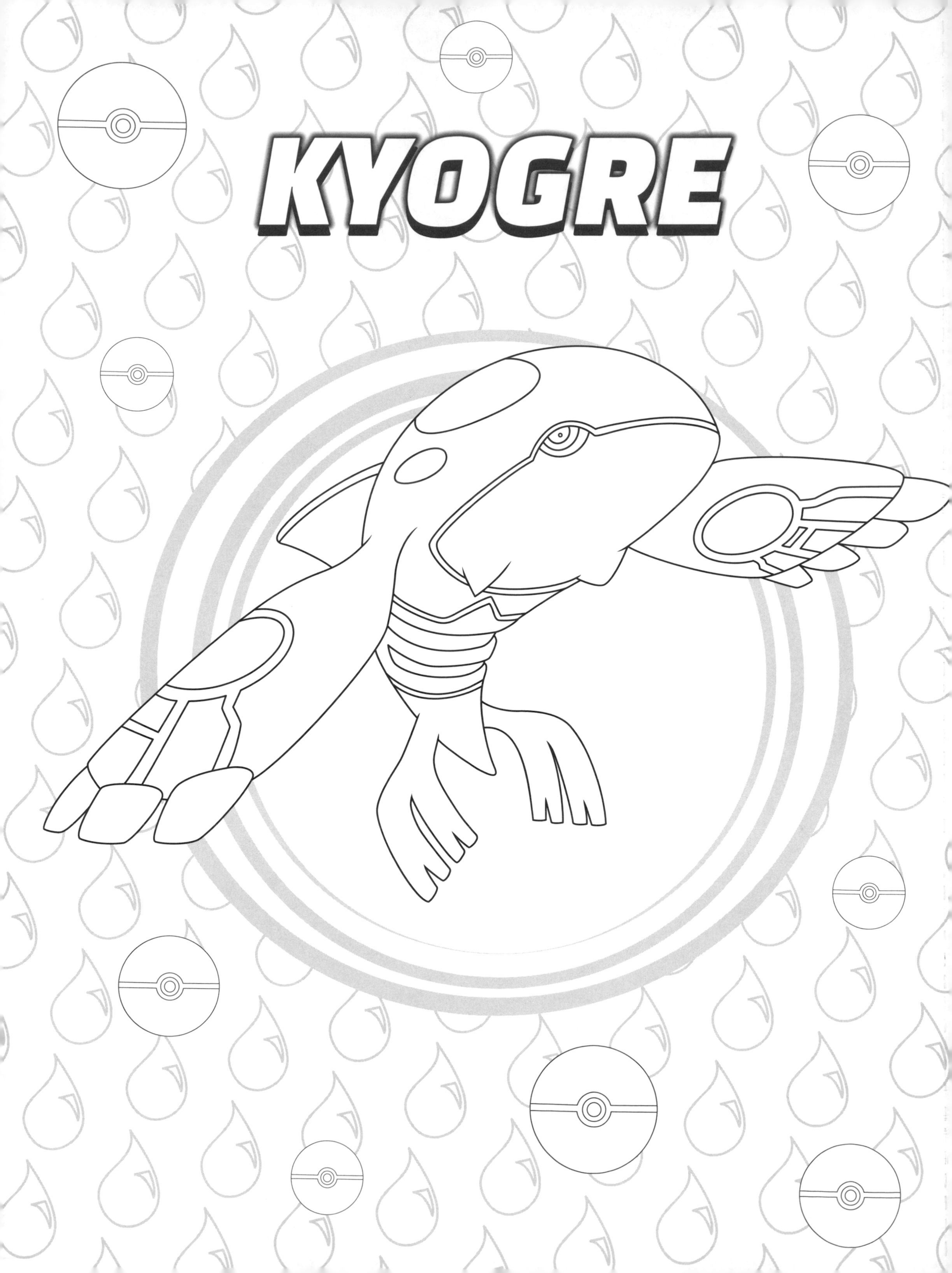
KYOGRE

DIANCIE
MEGA DIANCIE

HOOPA

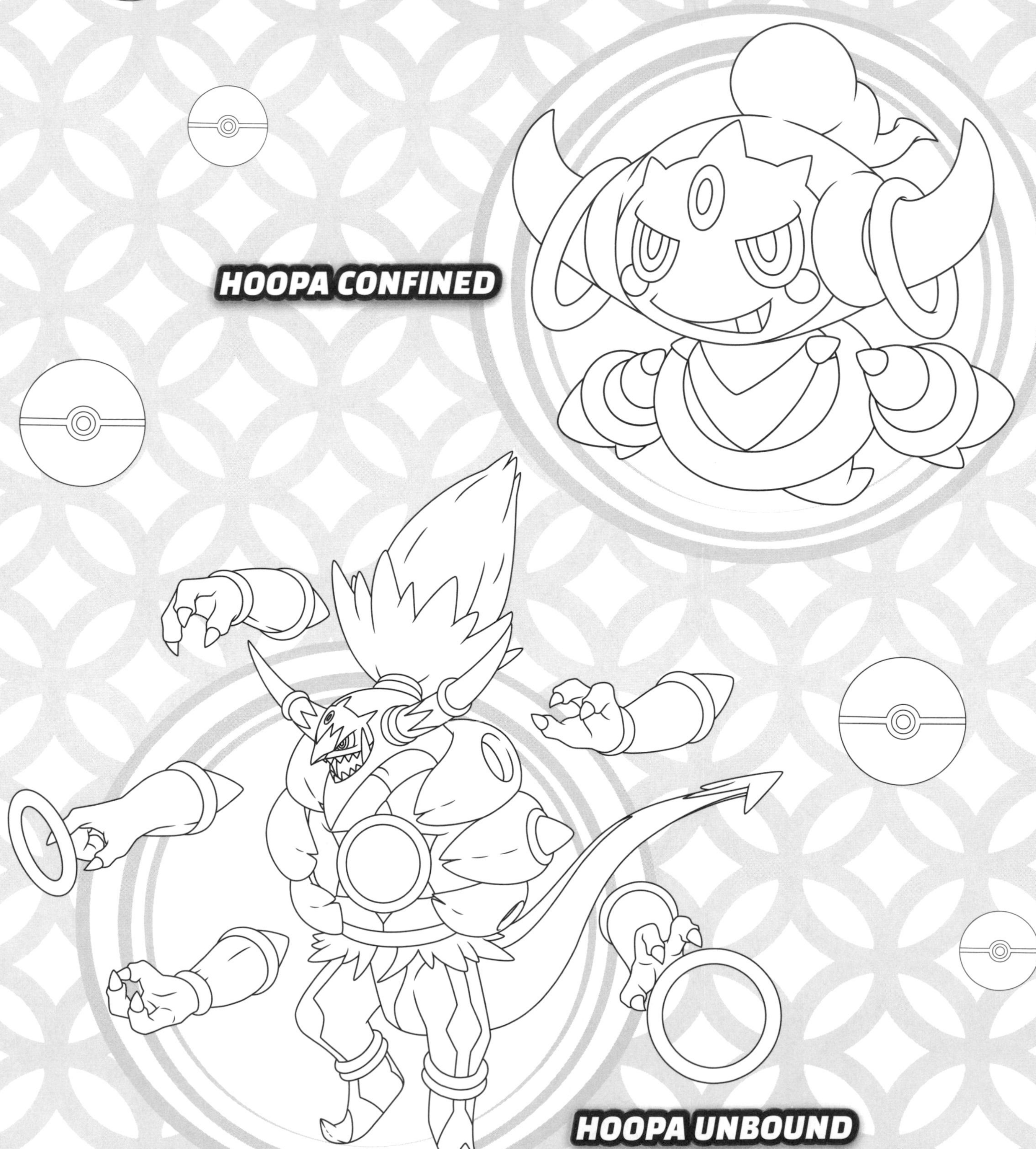

GROUDON

MANAPHY

ARTICUNO
MOLTRES
ZAPDOS

REGISTEEL

SHAYMIN

LAND FORME

SKY FORME

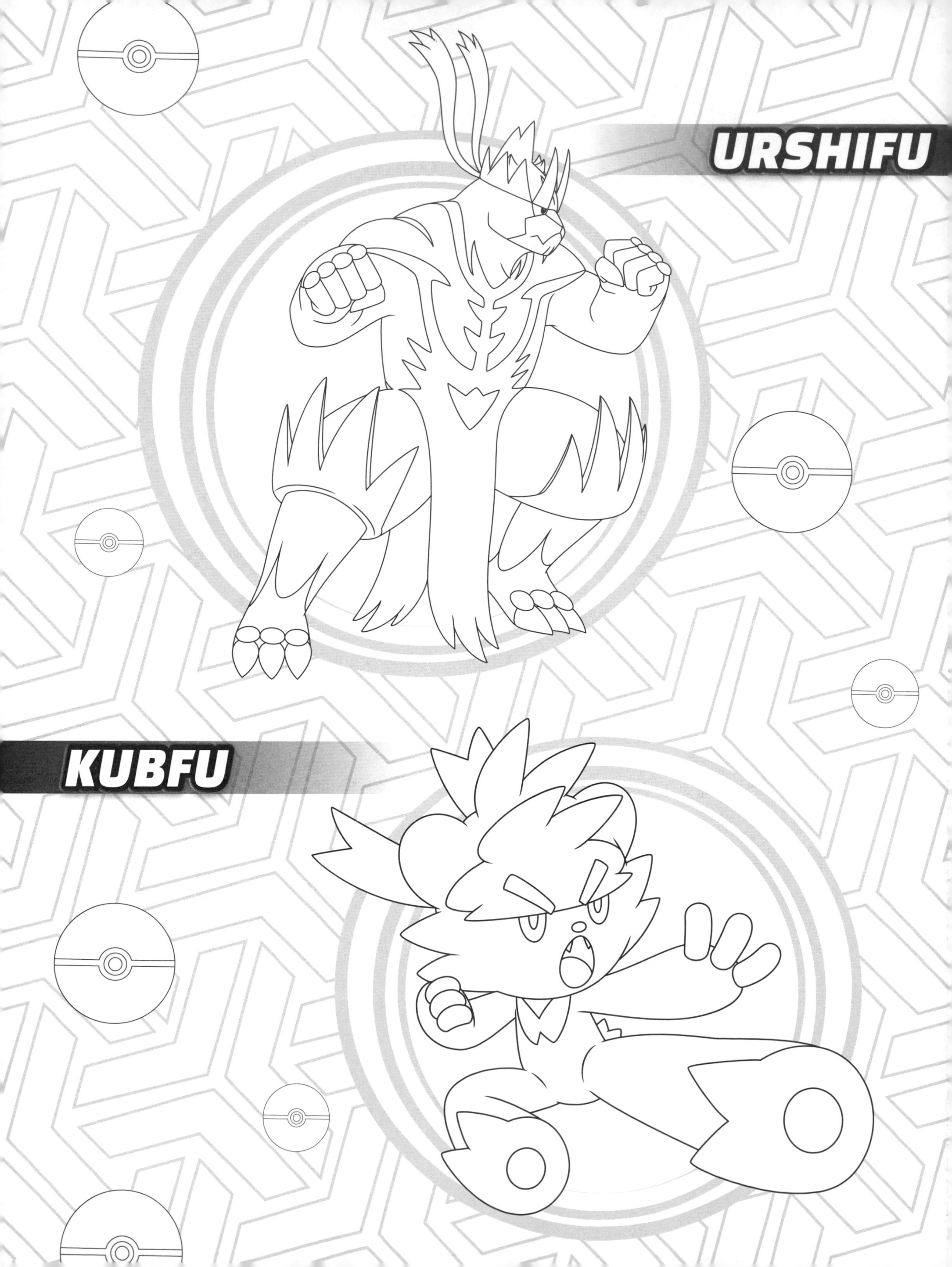
URSHIFU
KUBFU

MOLTRES

TORNADUS

INCARNATE FORME

THERIAN FORME

VICTINI

ARTICUNO

THUNDURUS

THERIAN FORME

GENESECT

LANDORUS

INCARNATE FORME

THERIAN FORME

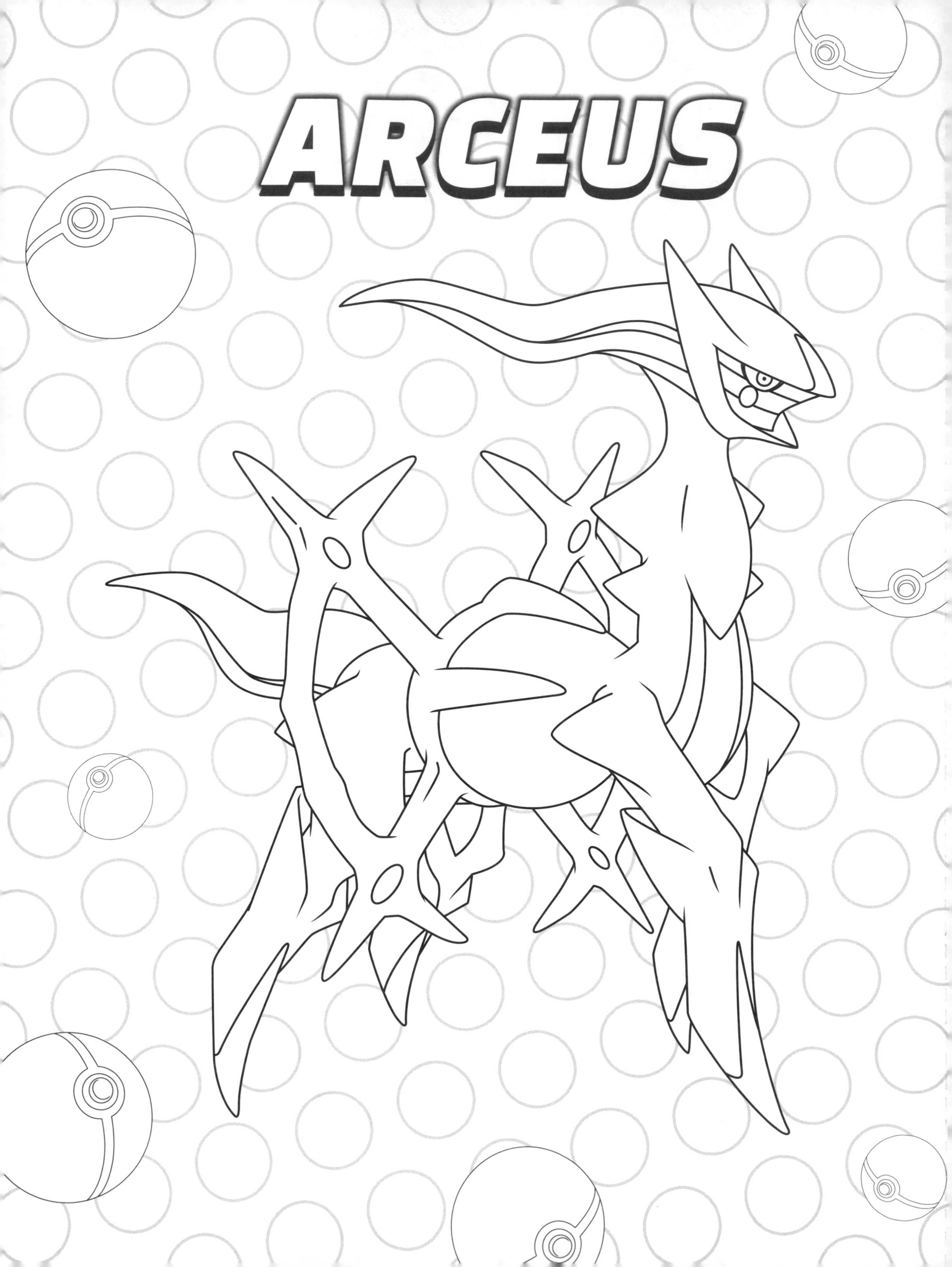
ARCEUS

CELEBI

ENTEI

MANAPHY
PHIONE

HO-OH
LUGIA

SUICUNE

DIALGA

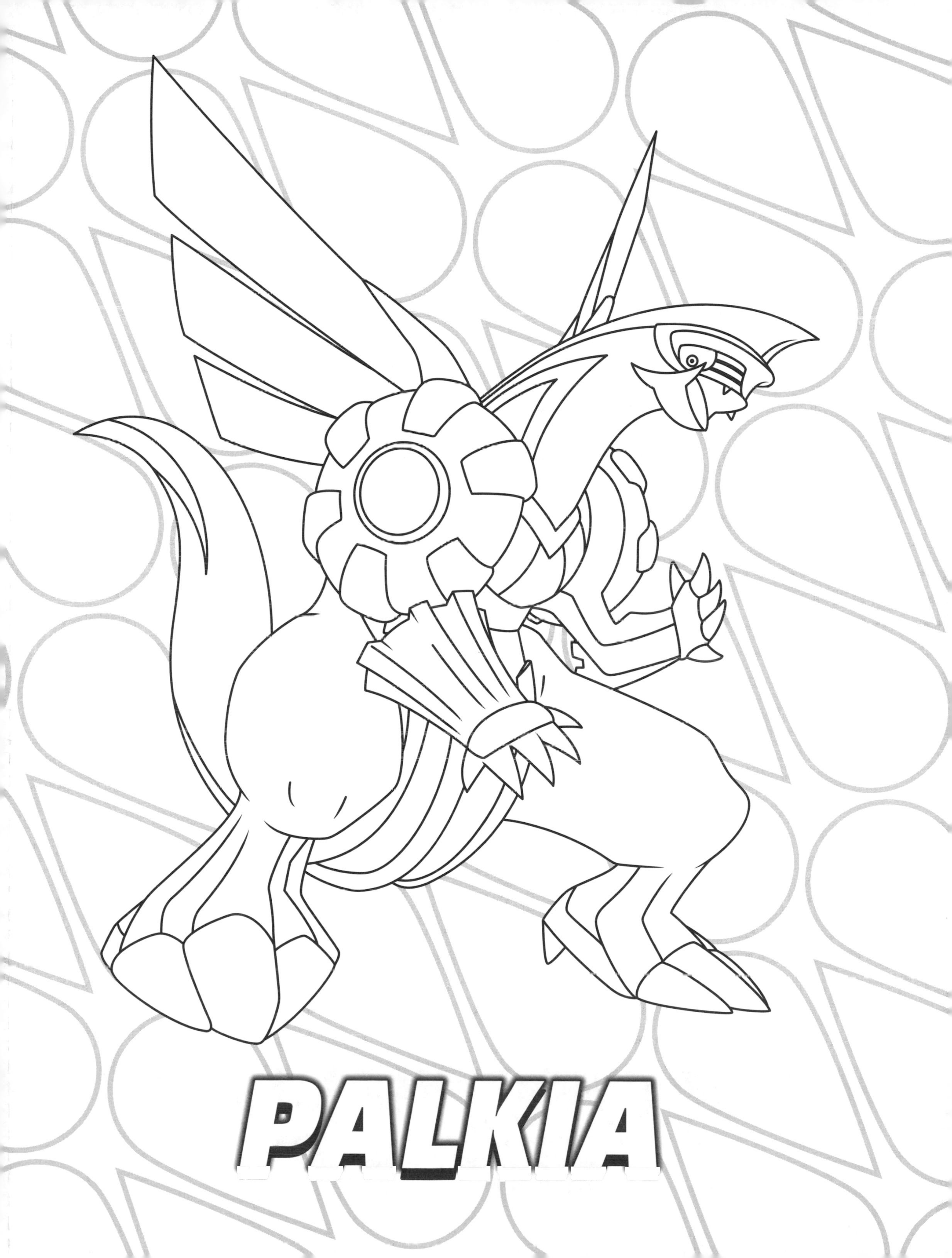
PALKIA

COBALION

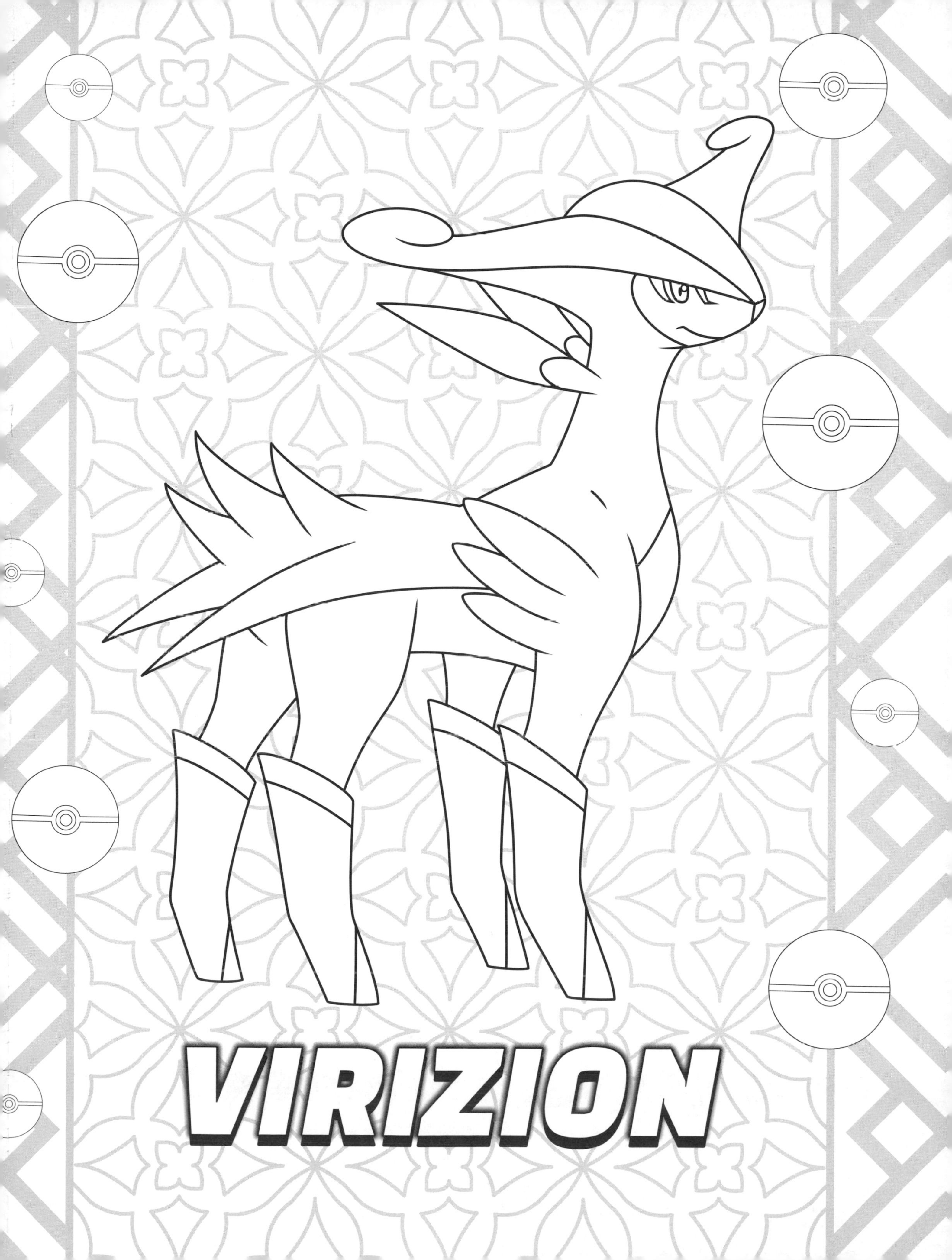
VIRIZION

TERRAKION

KELDEO

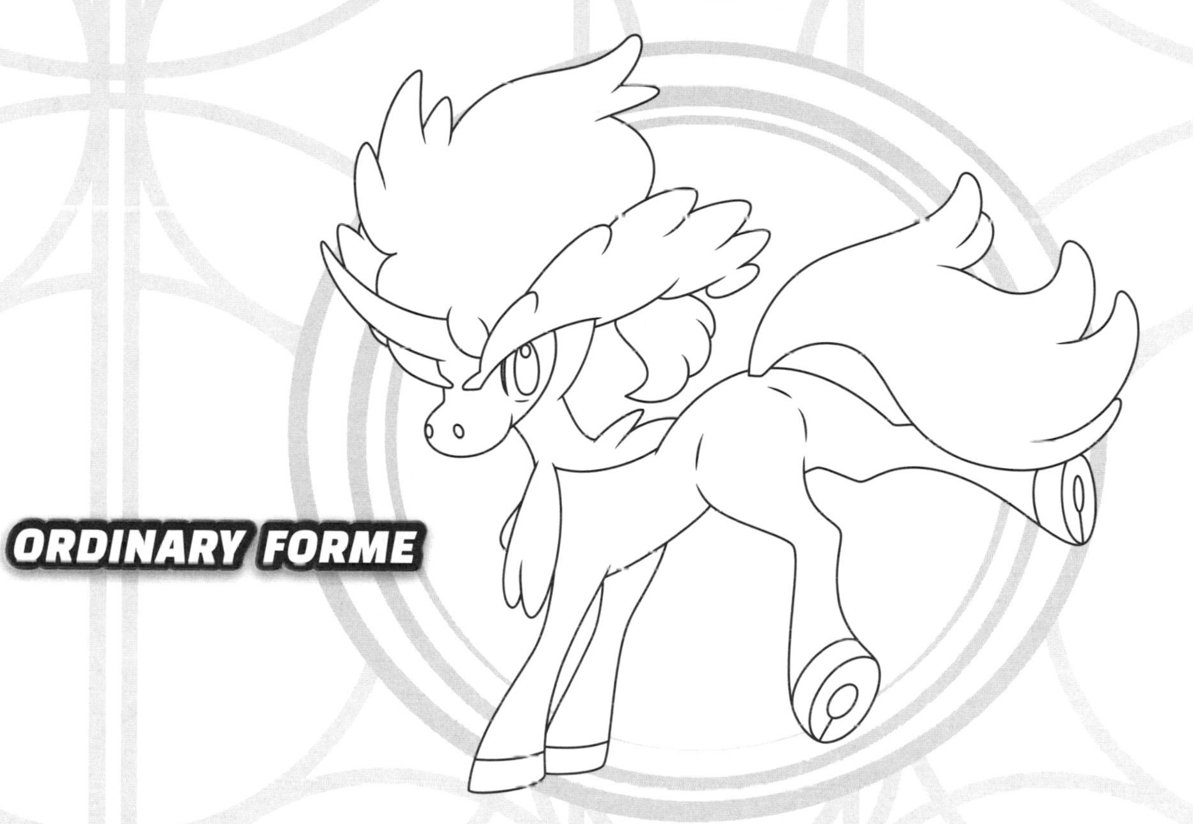

ORDINARY FORME

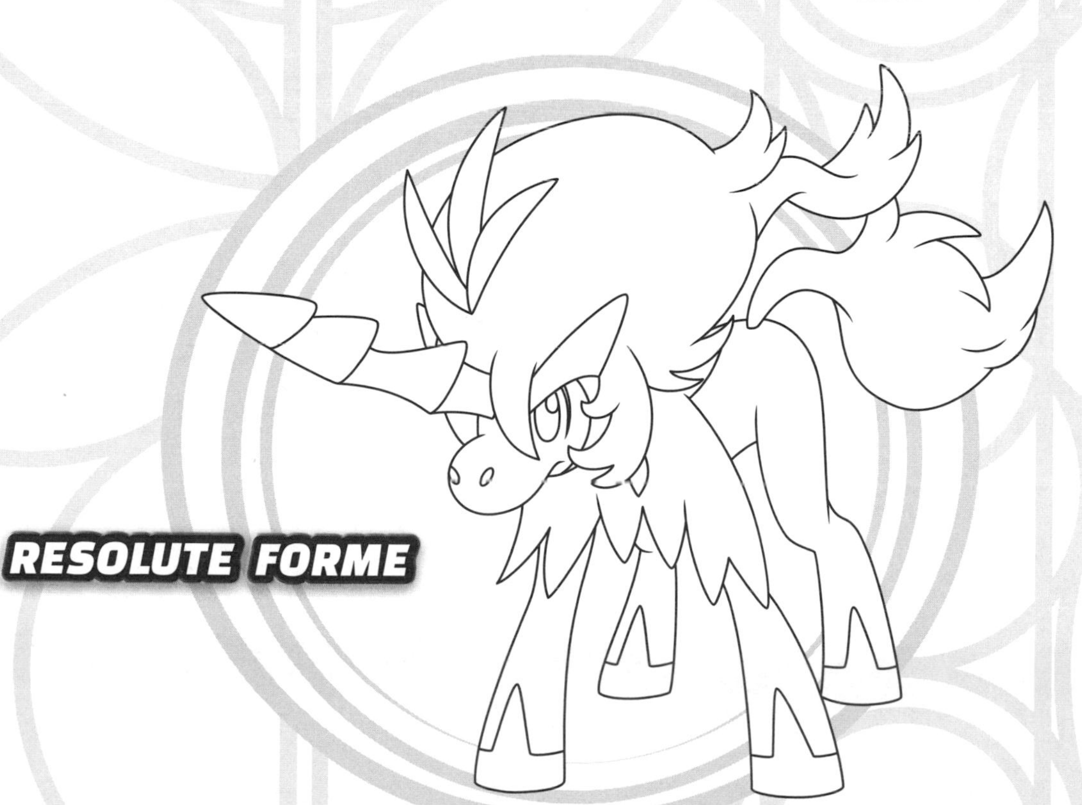

RESOLUTE FORME

REGIGIGAS

RAIKOU

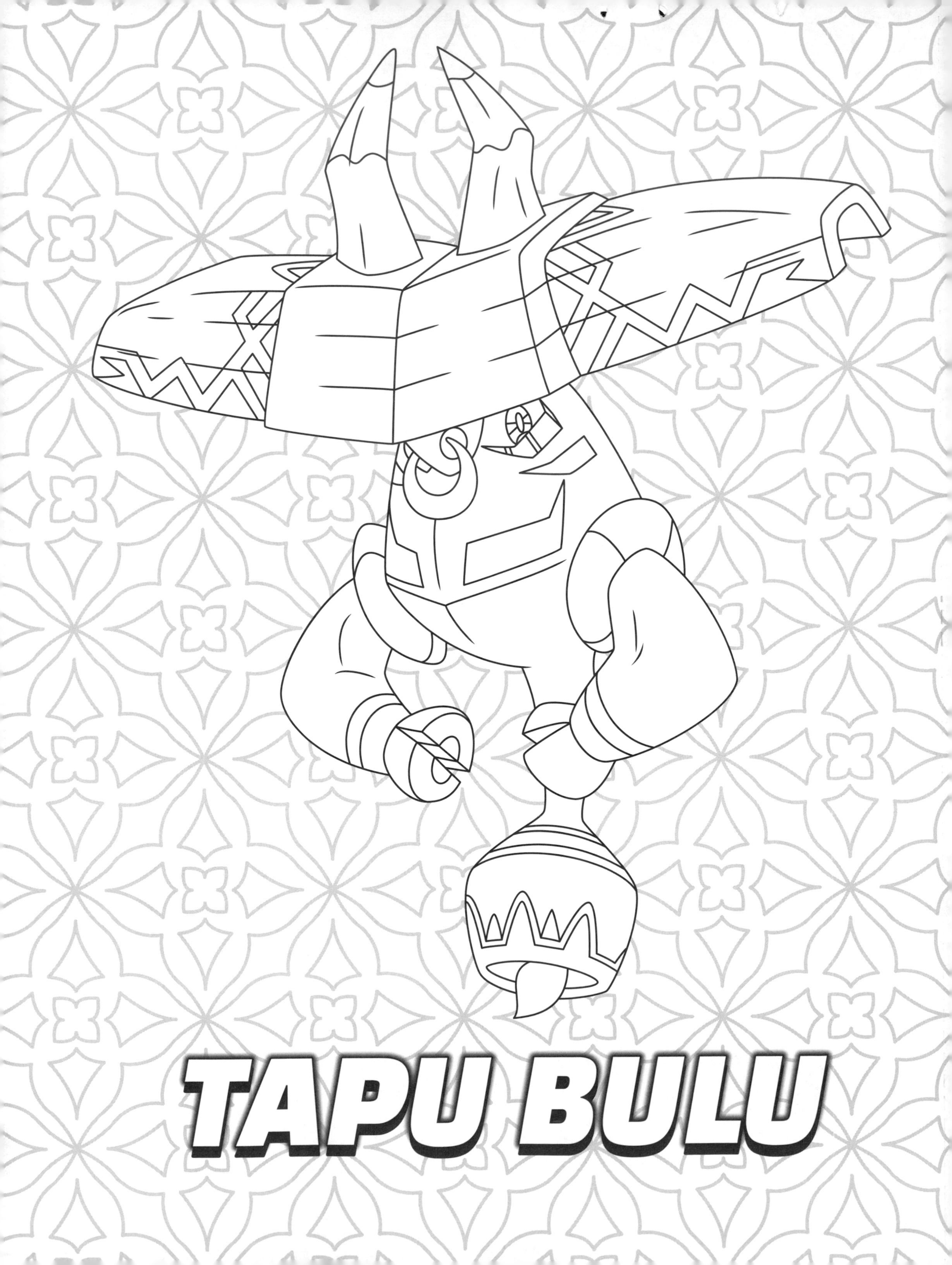
TAPU BULU

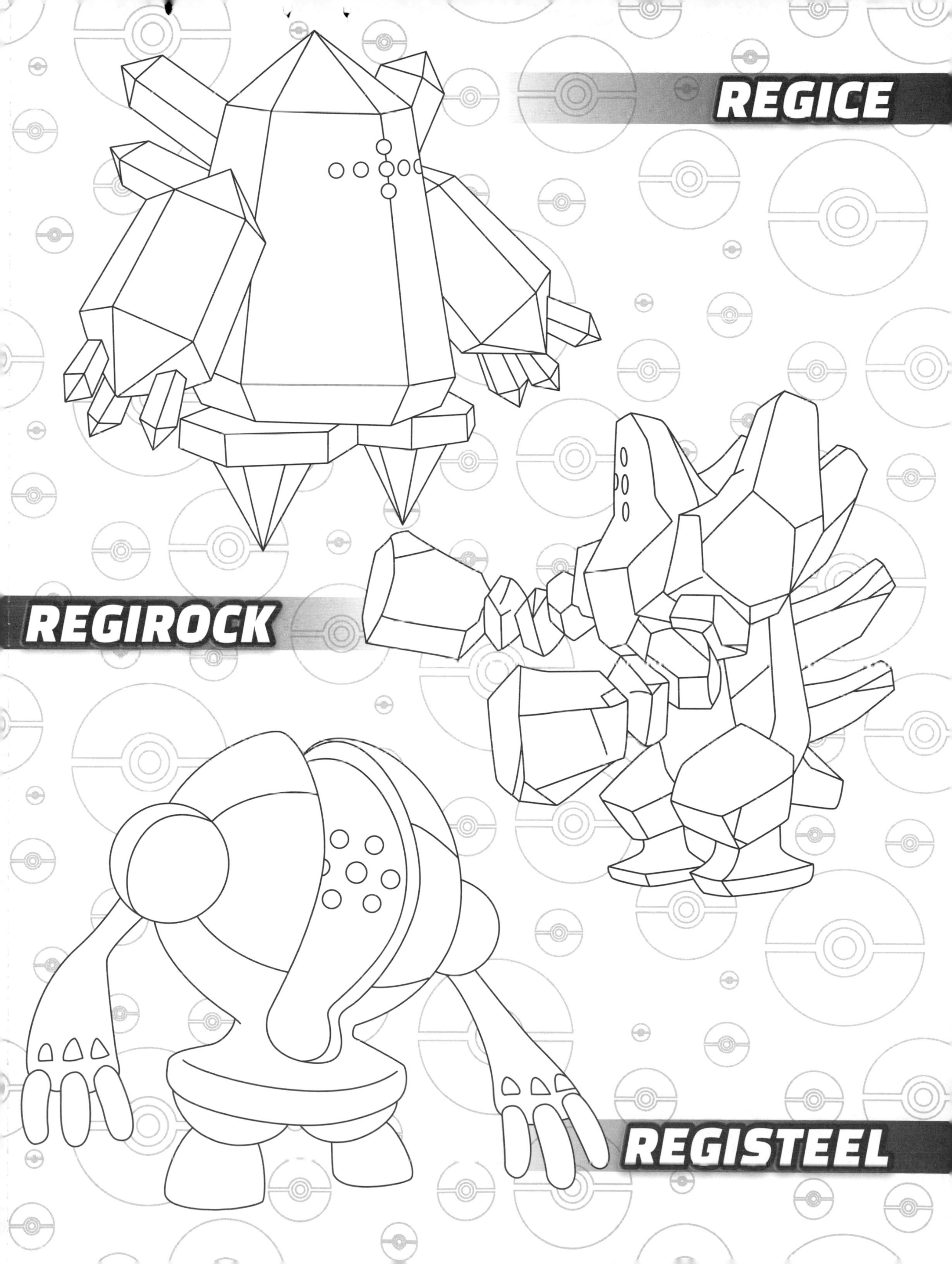
REGICE
REGIROCK
REGISTEEL

MAGEARNA

MARSHADOW
ZENITH MARSHADOW

THUNDURUS
TORNADUS
LANDORUS

MELMETAL
MELTAN

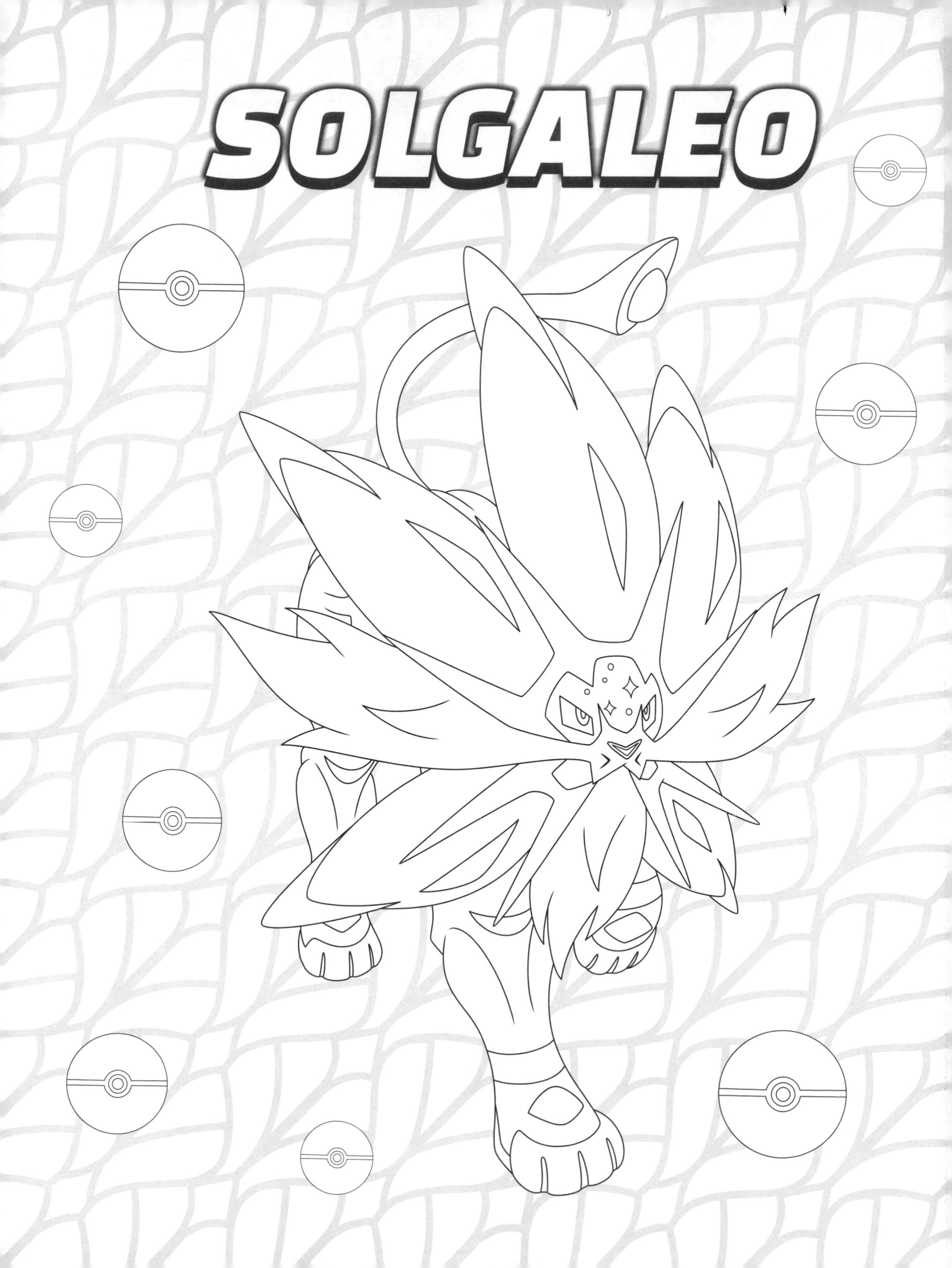
SOLGALEO

LUNALA

RESHIRAM

XERNEAS
YVELTAL
ZYGARDE 50%

MELOETTA
ARIA FORME
PIROUETTE FORME

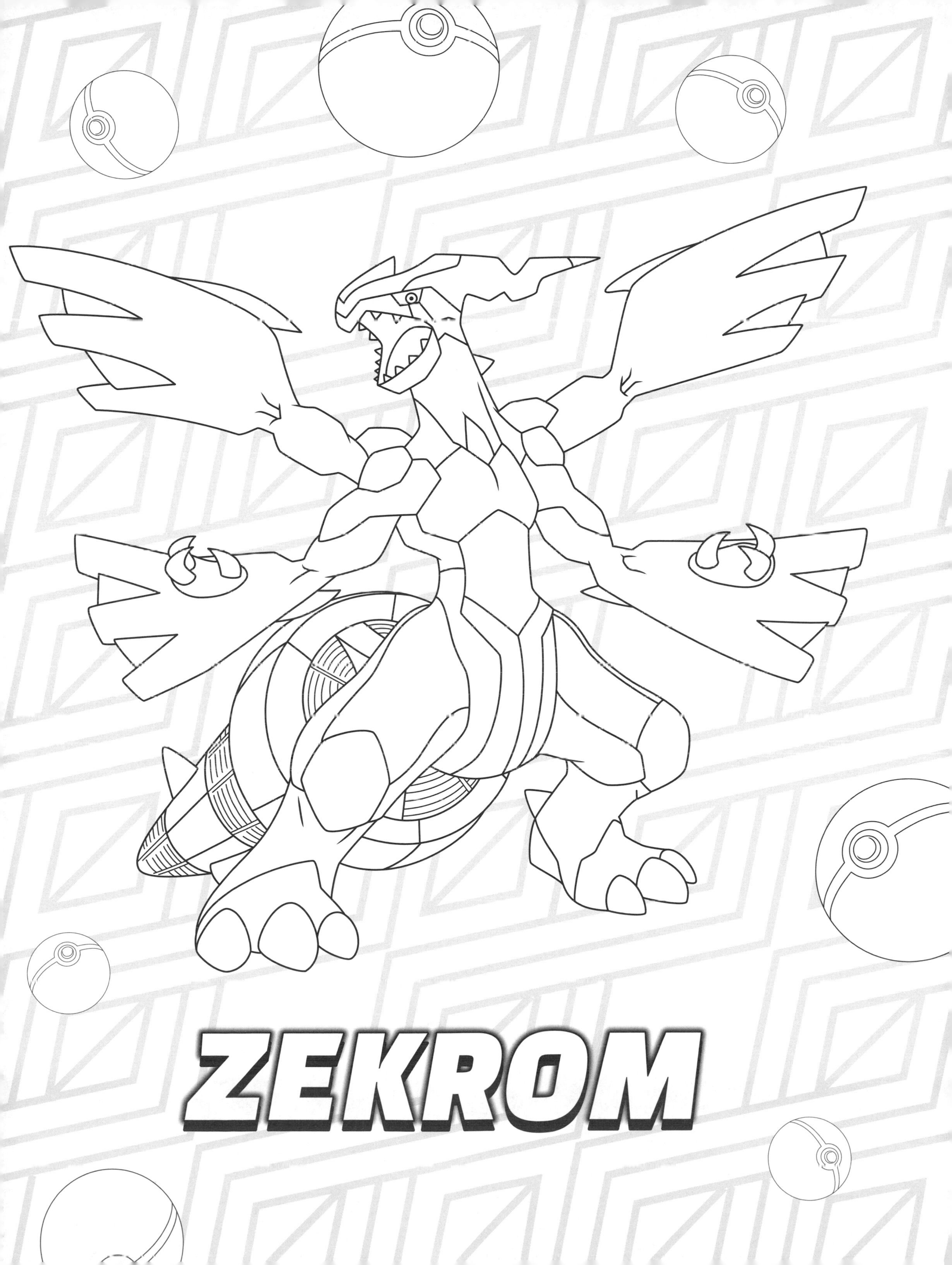
ZEKROM

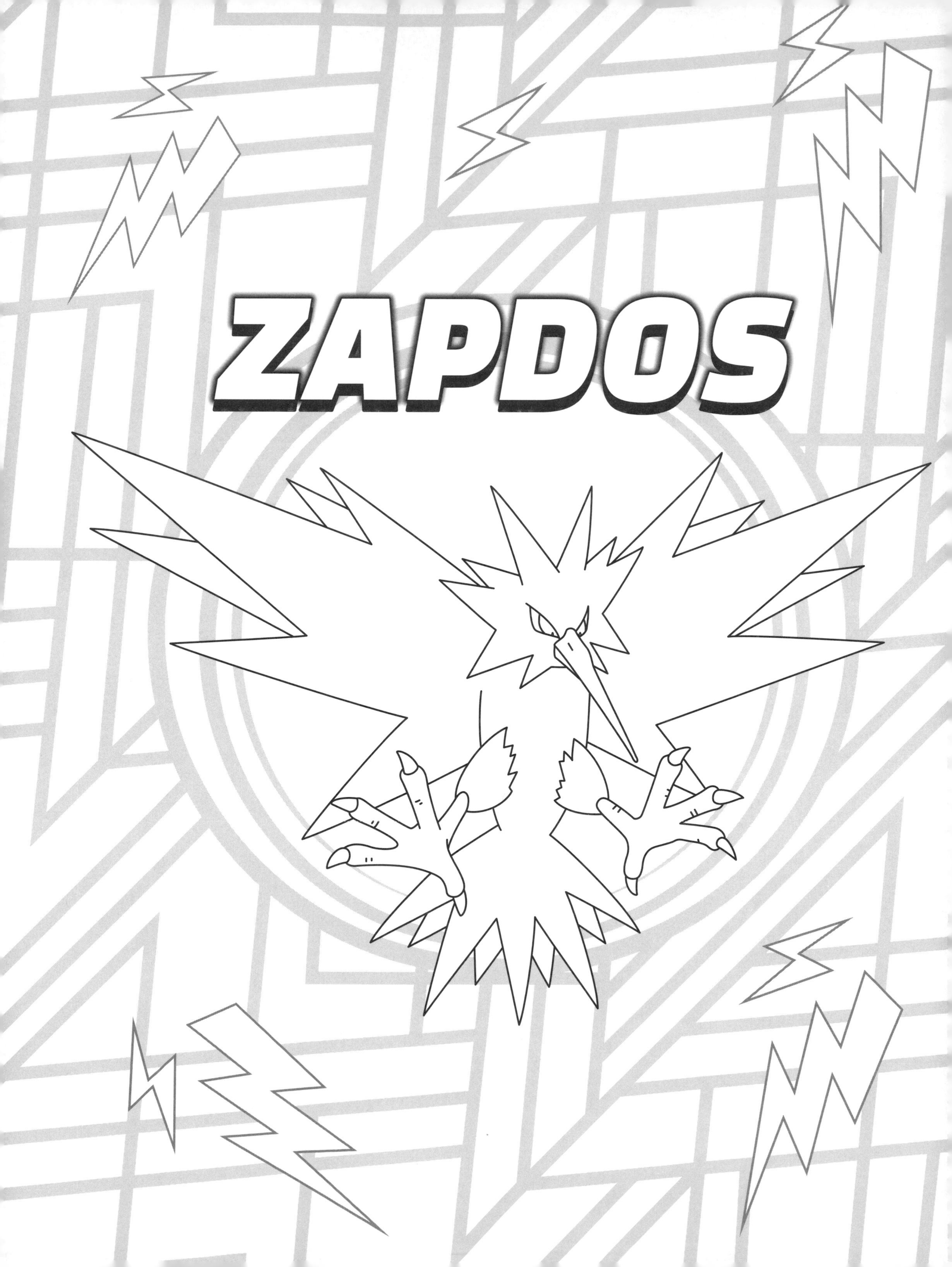
ZAPDOS

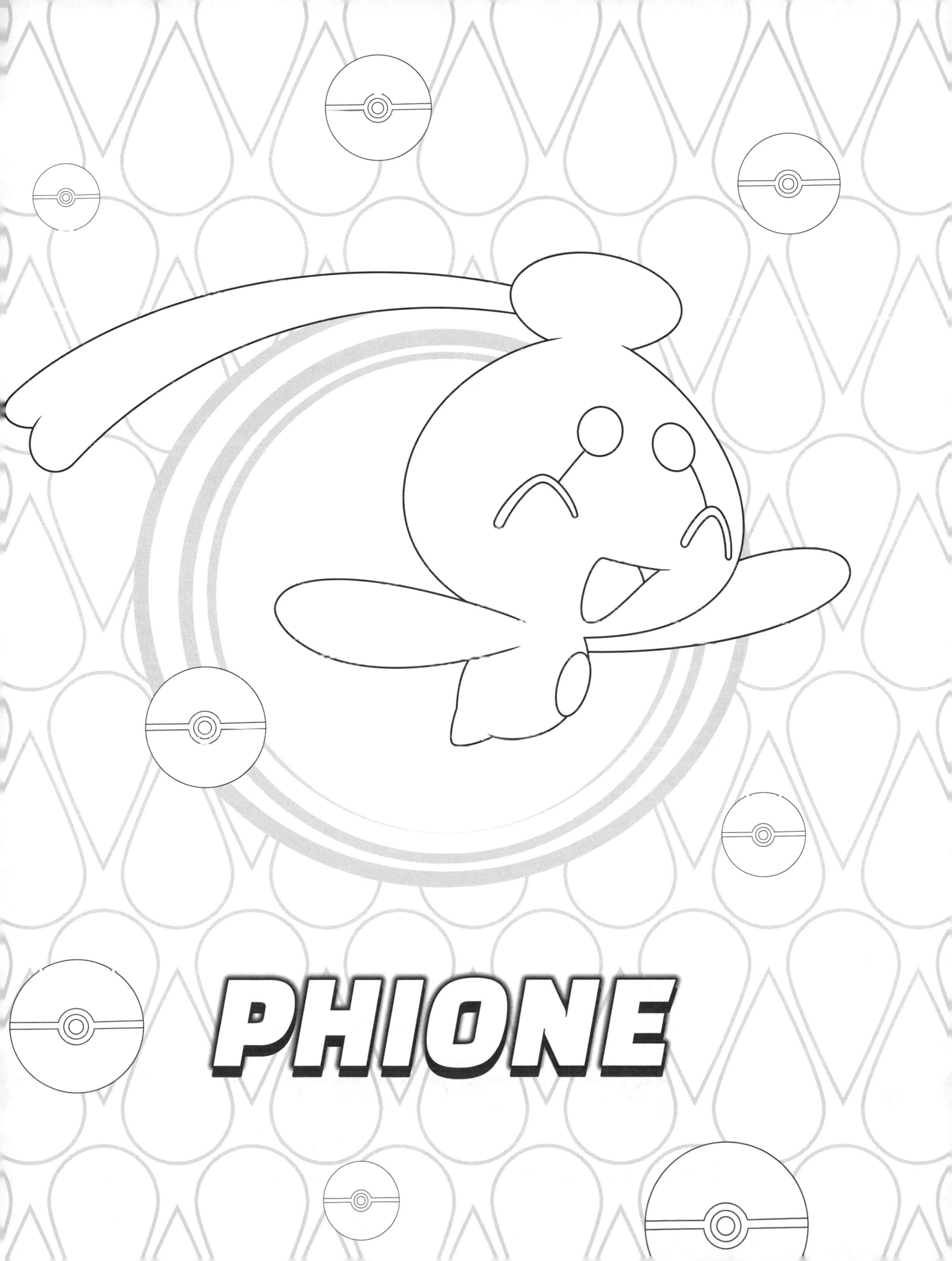
PHIONE

DARKRAI

HEATRAN

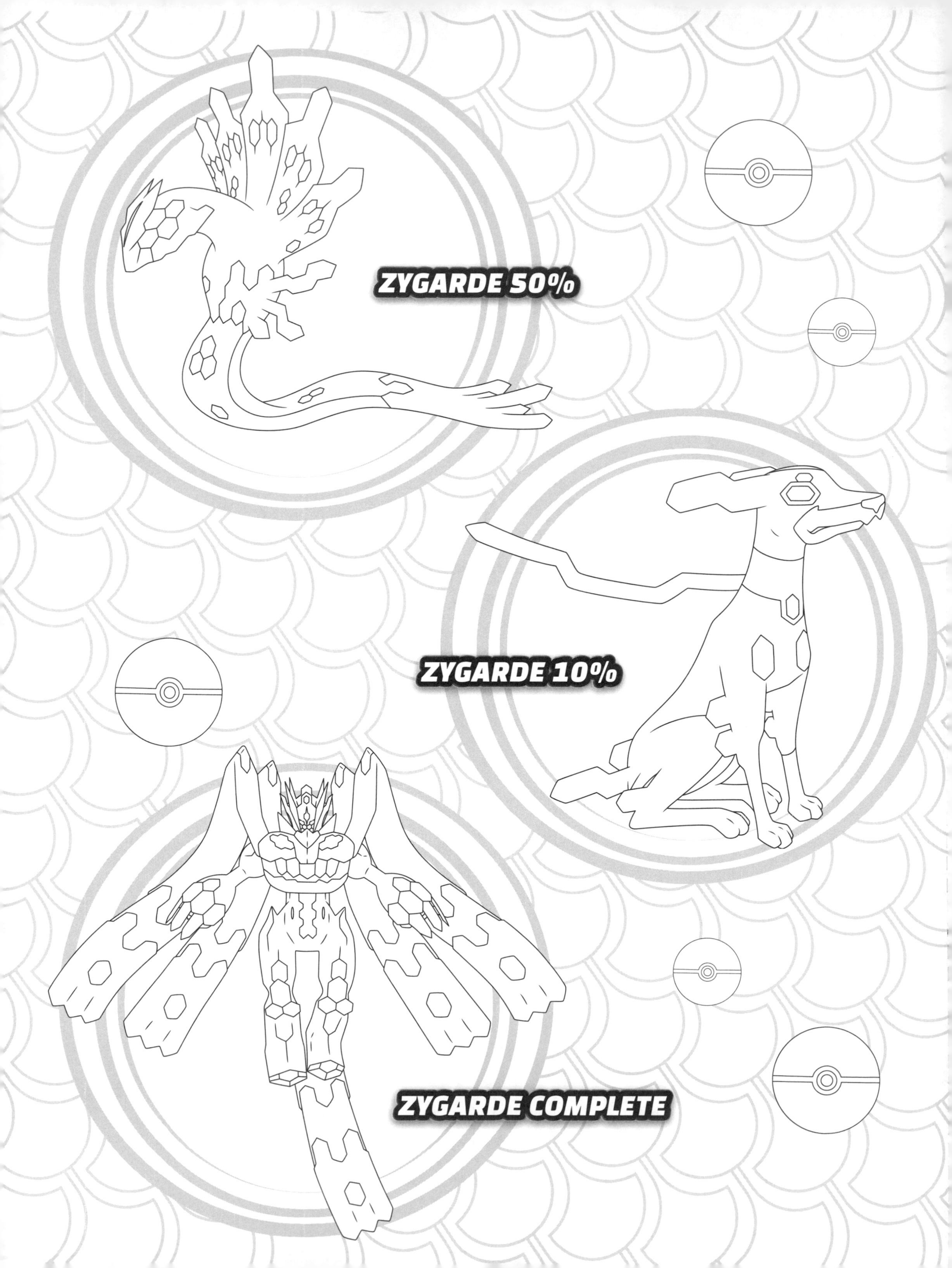
ZYGARDE 50%
ZYGARDE 10%
ZYGARDE COMPLETE

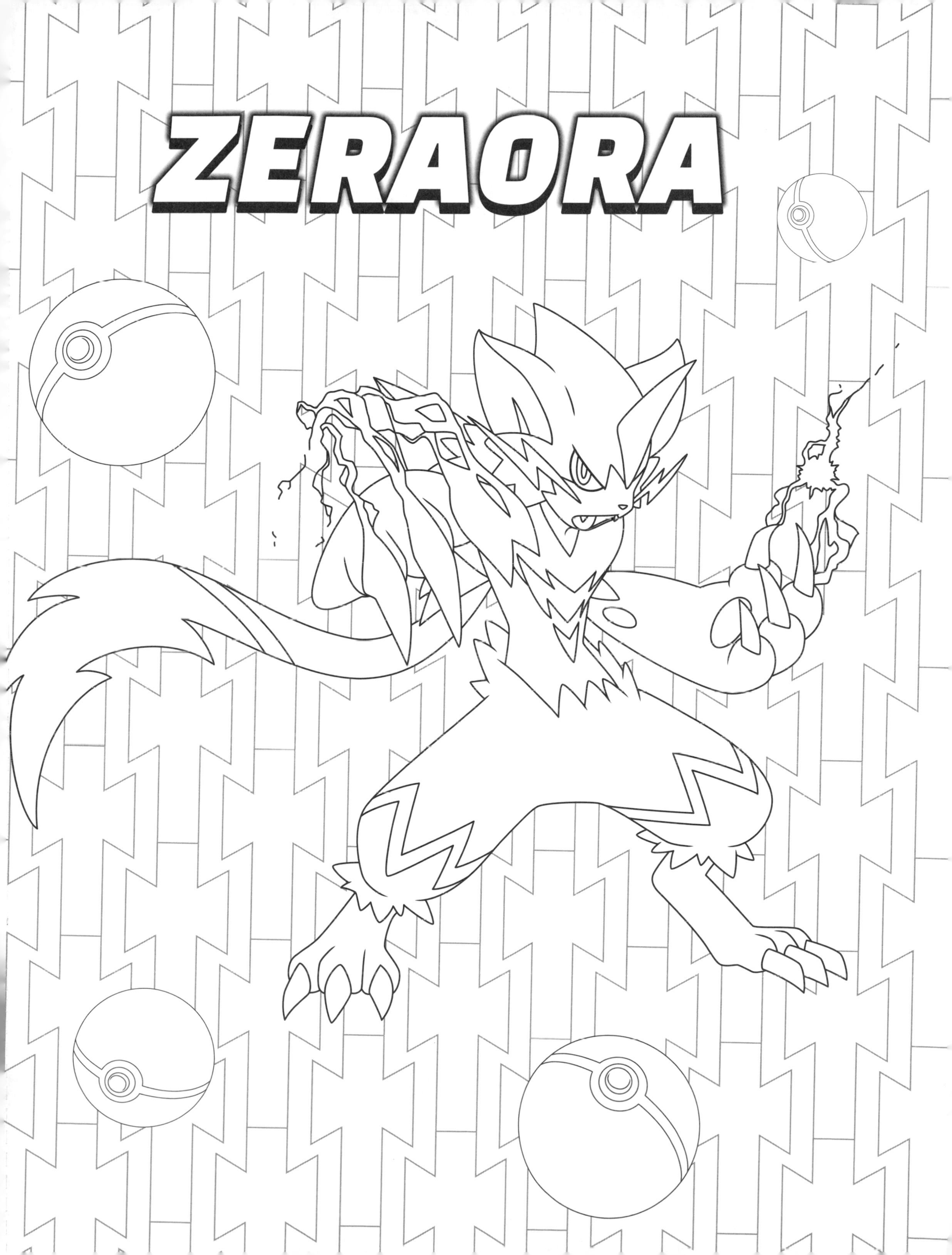
ZERAORA

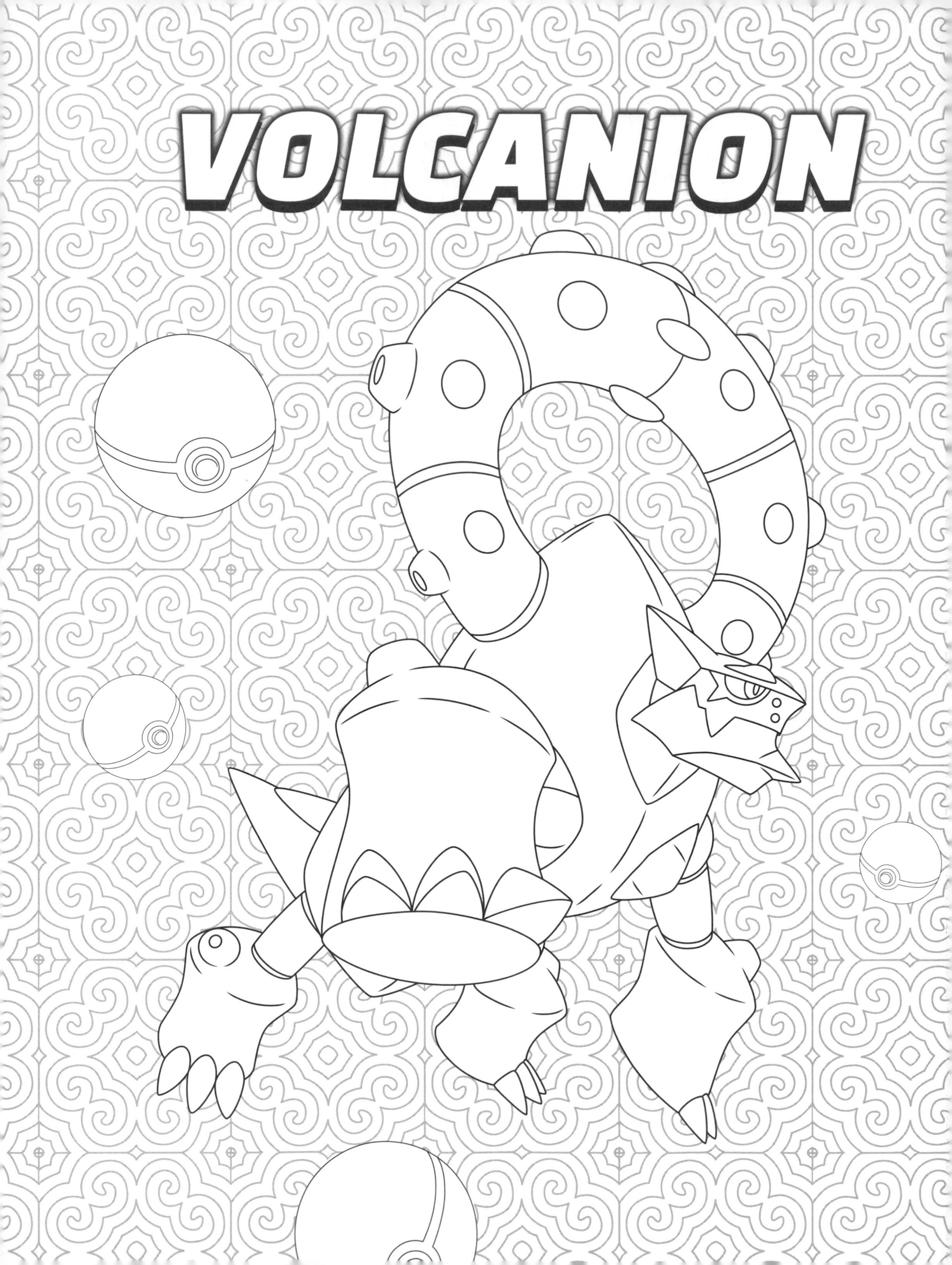
VOLCANION

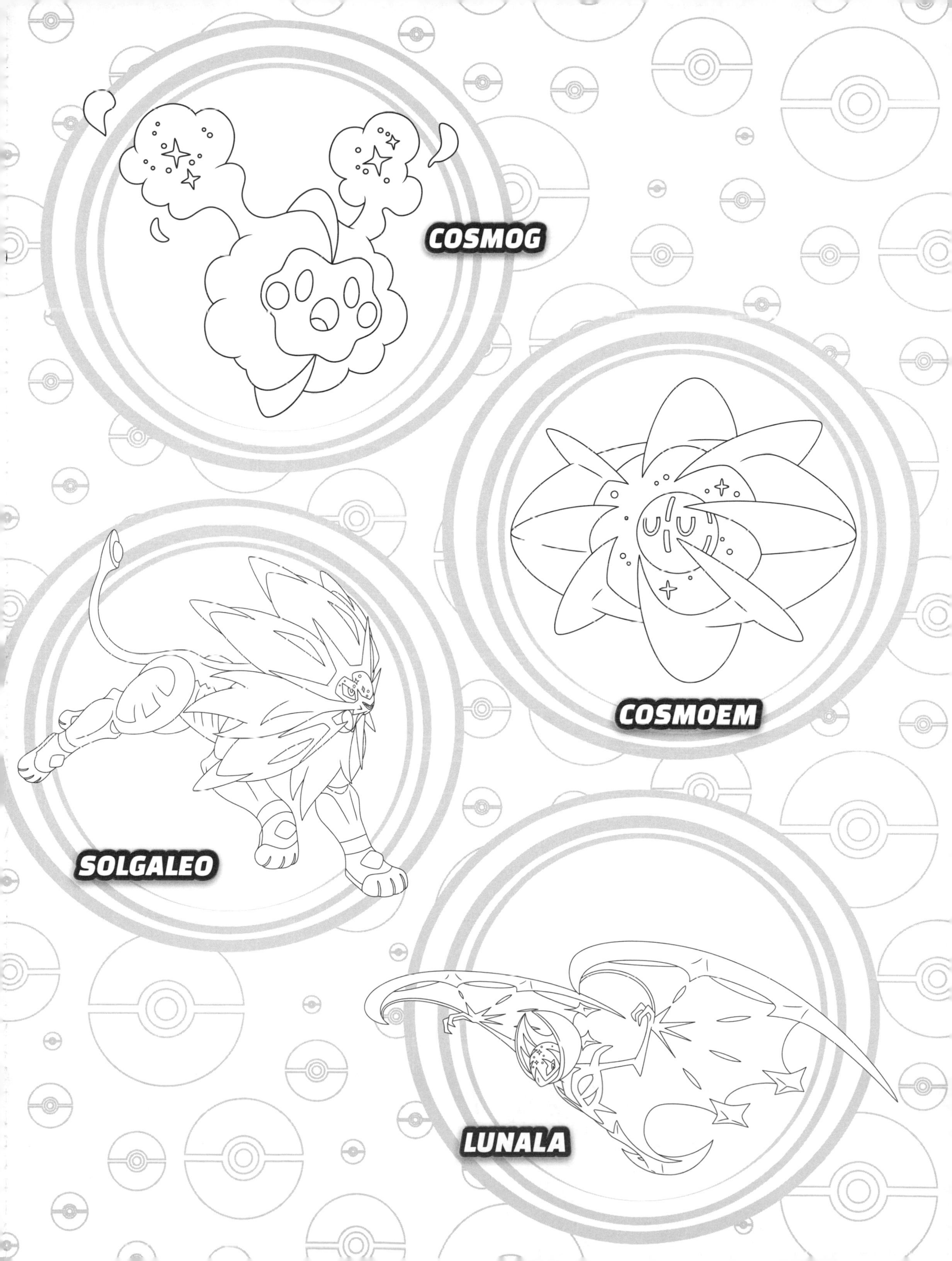
COSMOG
COSMOEM
SOLGALEO
LUNALA

TAPU KOKO

COSMOEM

AZELF
MESPRIT
UXIE

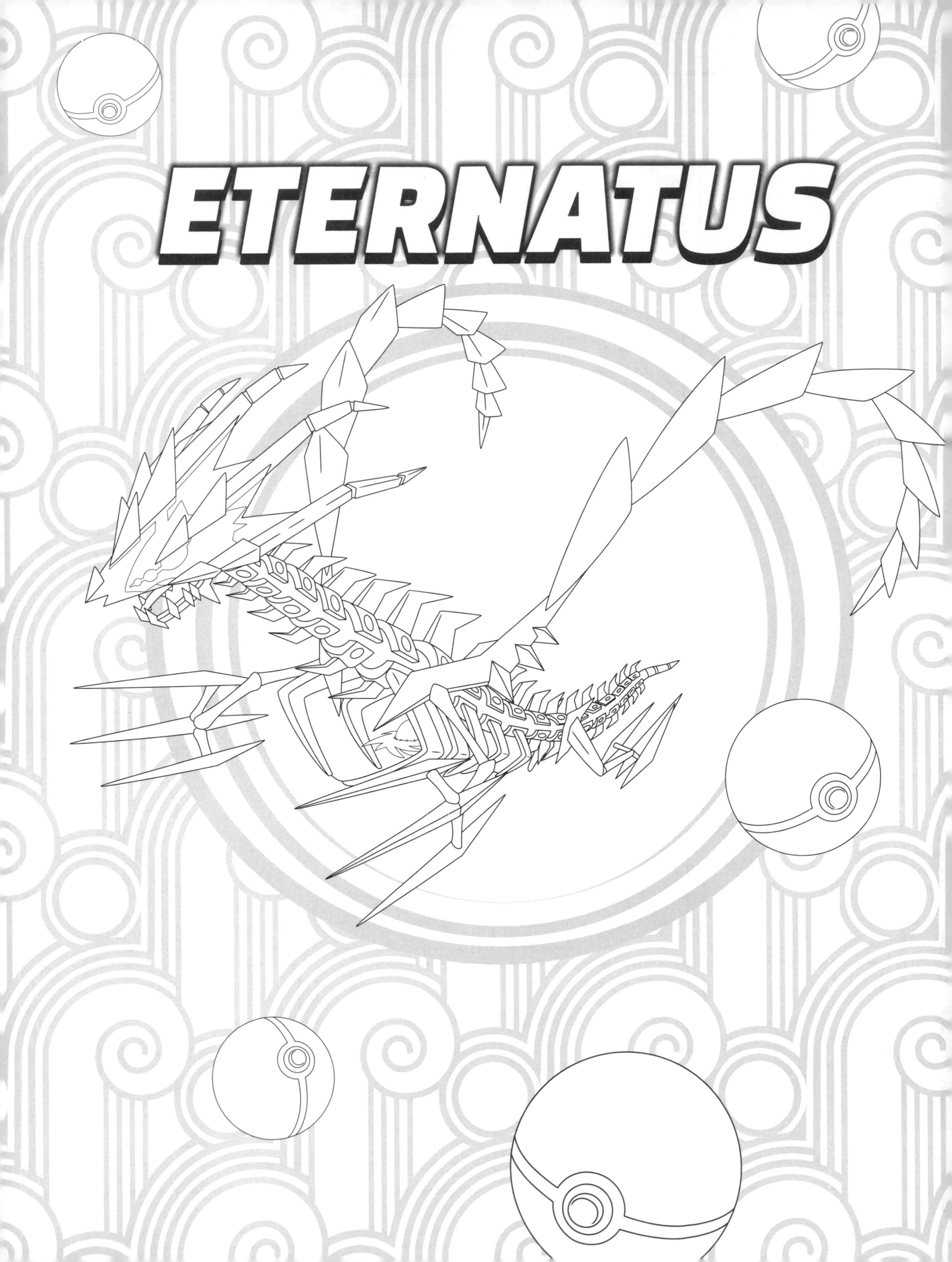
ETERNATUS

KUBFU

TYPE: NULL
SILVALLY

CROWNED SWORD

ZEKROM
RESHIRAM
KYUREM

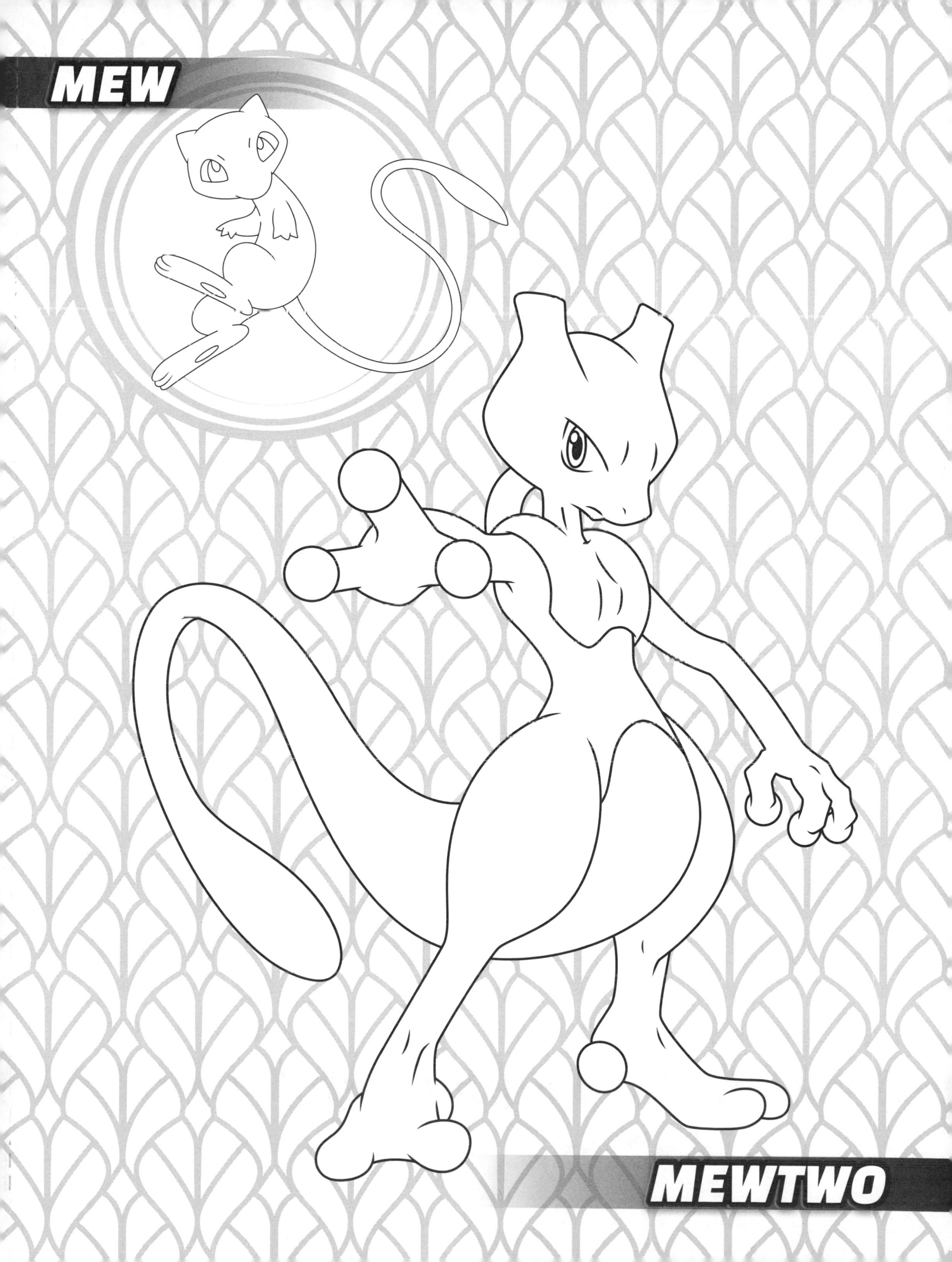
MEW
MEWTWO

TAPU FINI

MEW

CRESSELIA

ORIGIN FORME

ALTERED FORME

GIRATINA

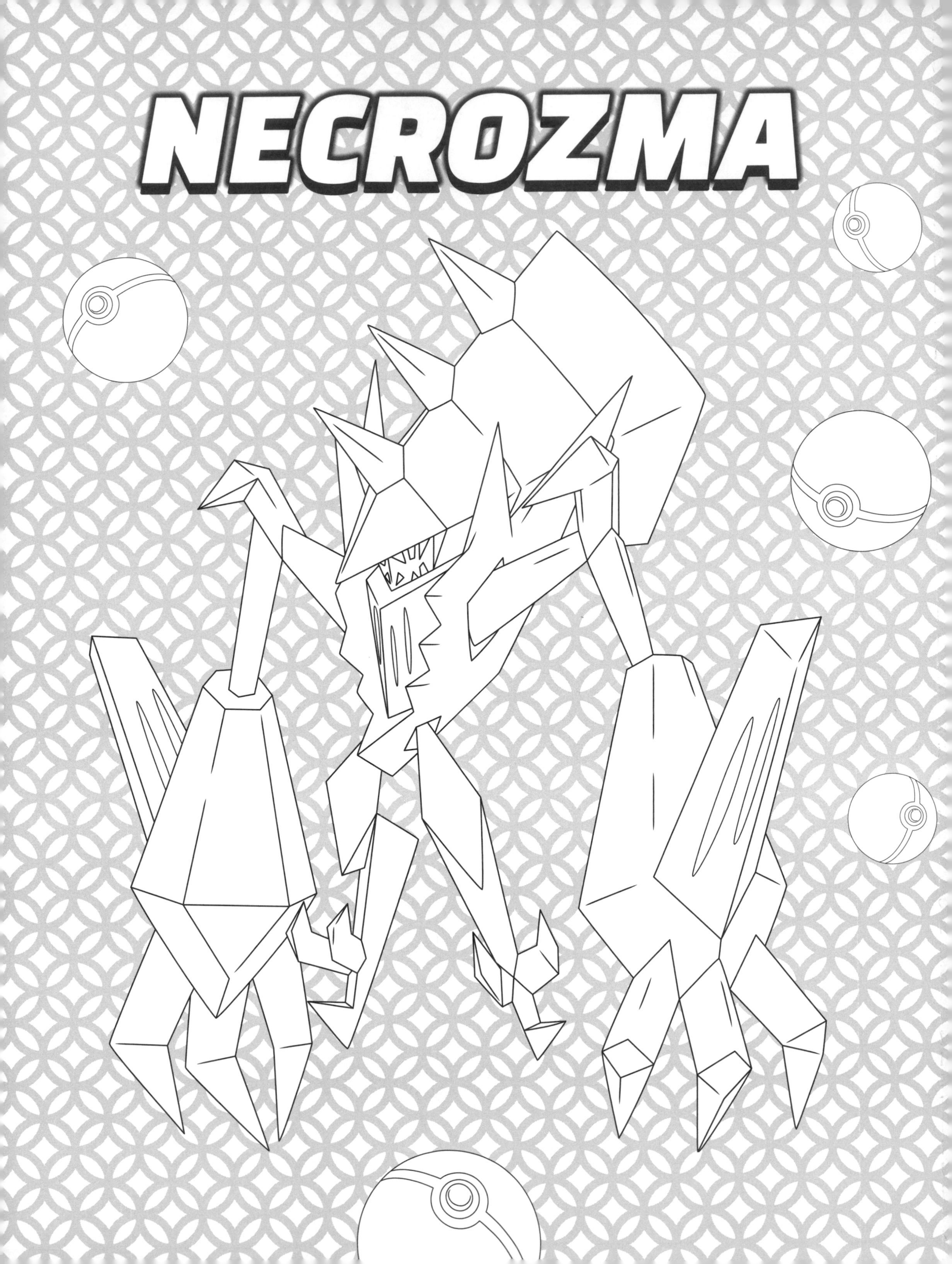
NECROZMA

DUSK MANE NECROZMA
DAWN WINGS NECROZMA
ULTRA NECROZMA

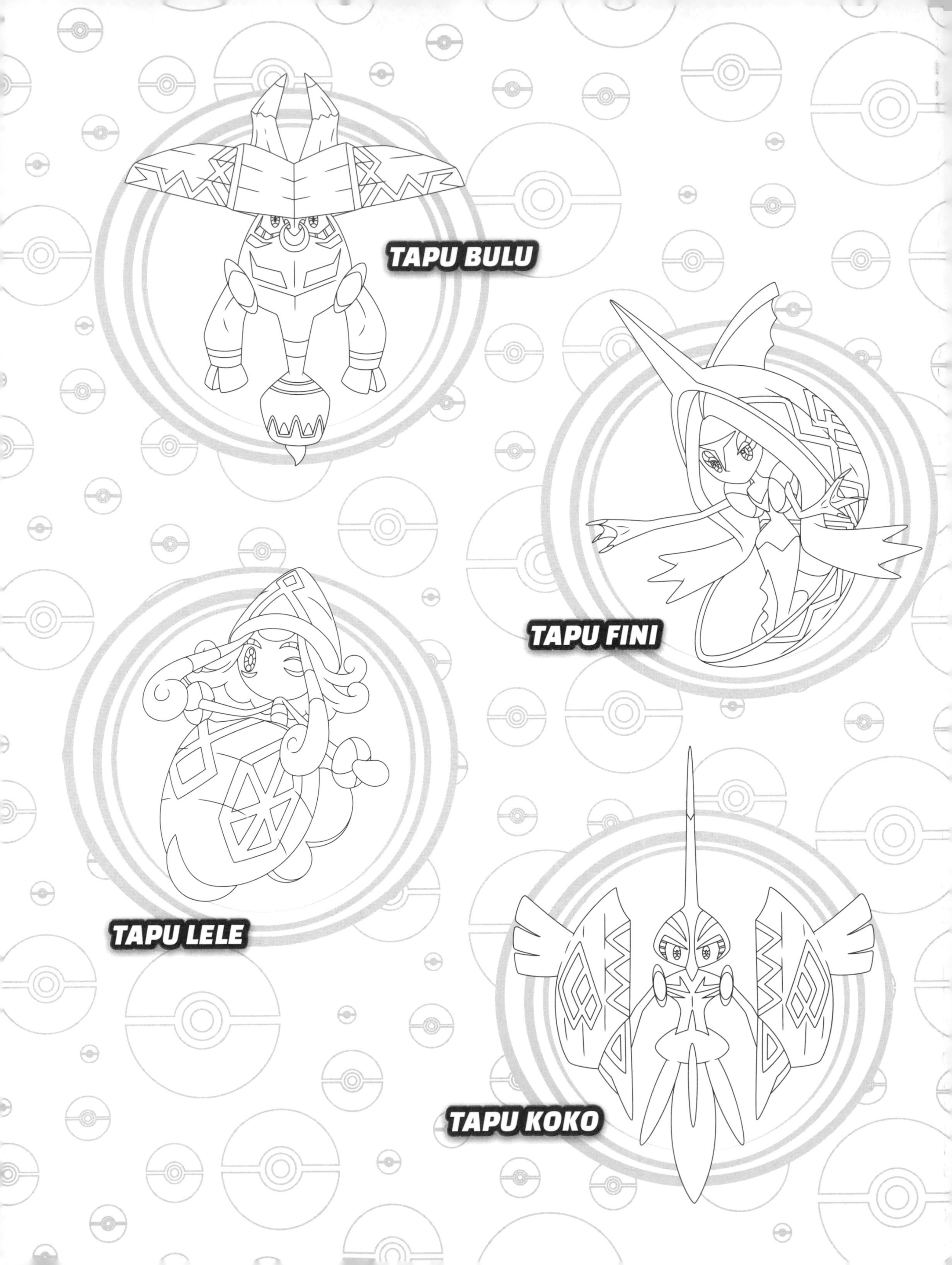
TAPU BULU
TAPU FINI
TAPU LELE
TAPU KOKO

KYOGRE
GROUDON

COSMOG

ZAMAZENTA

HERO OF MANY BATTLES

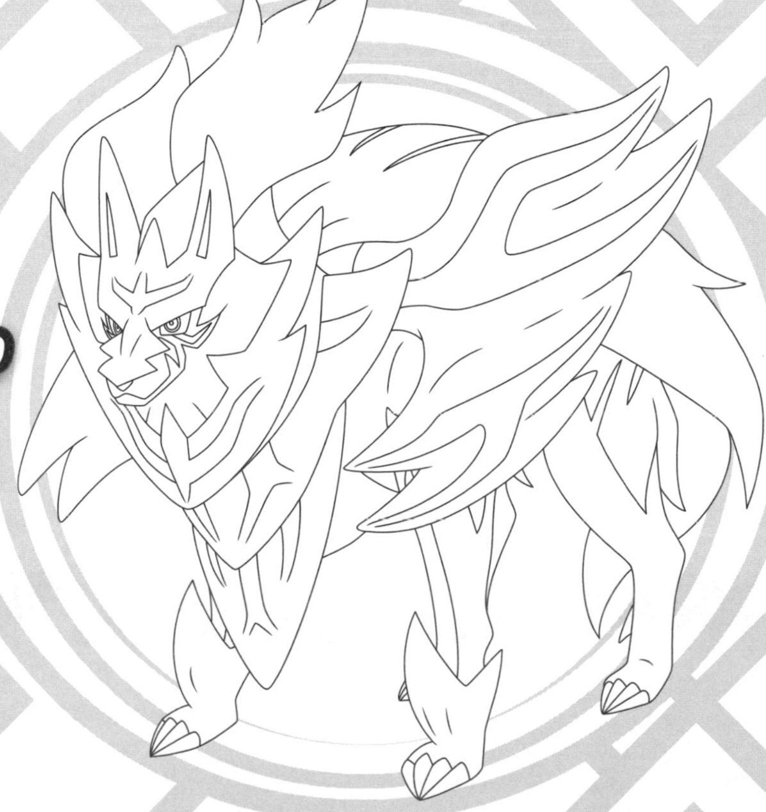

CROWNED SHIELD

YVELTAL

XERNEAS

ZACIAN
ZAMAZENTA

ZYGARDE 50%

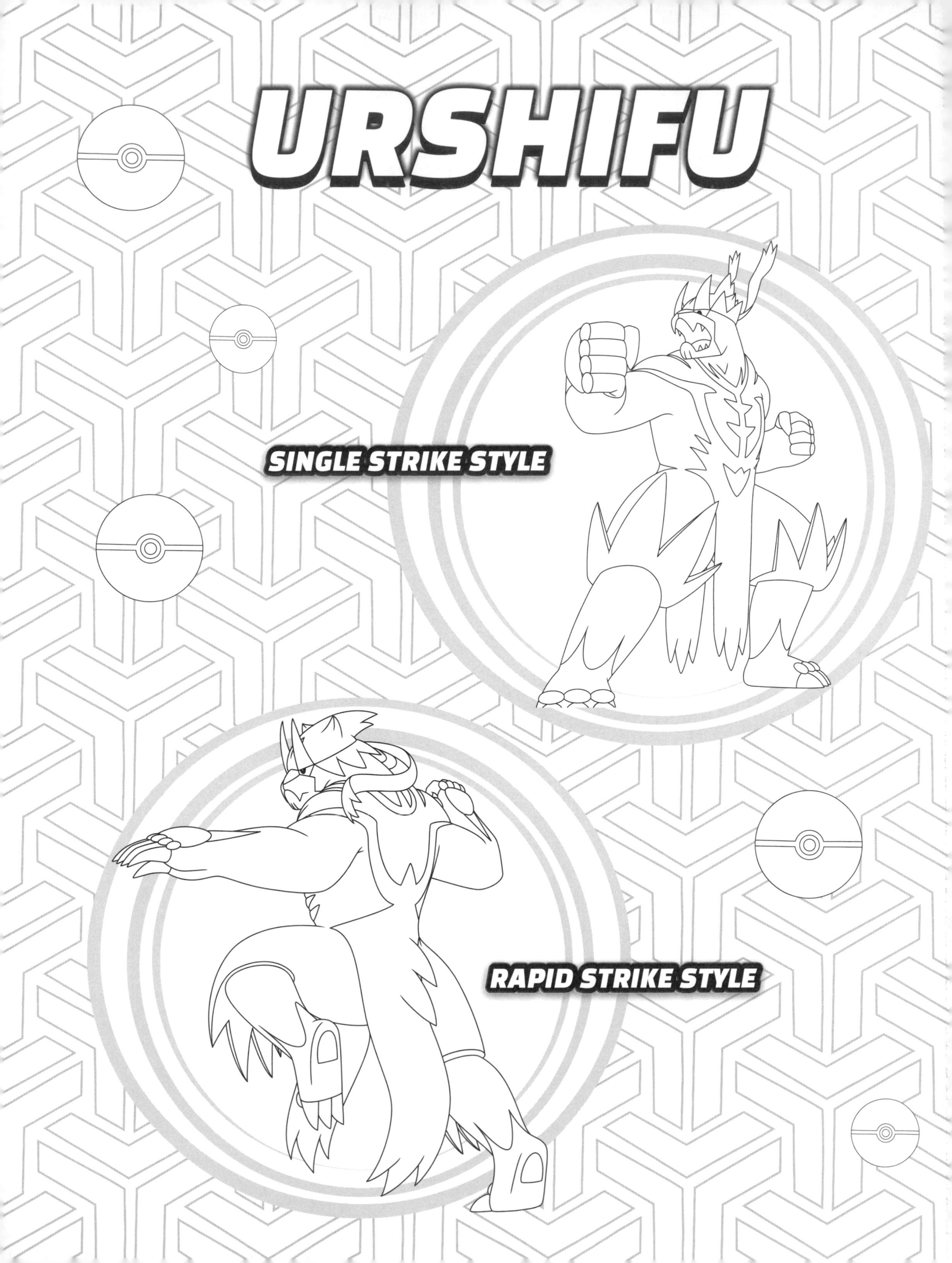
URSHIFU
SINGLE STRIKE STYLE
RAPID STRIKE STYLE

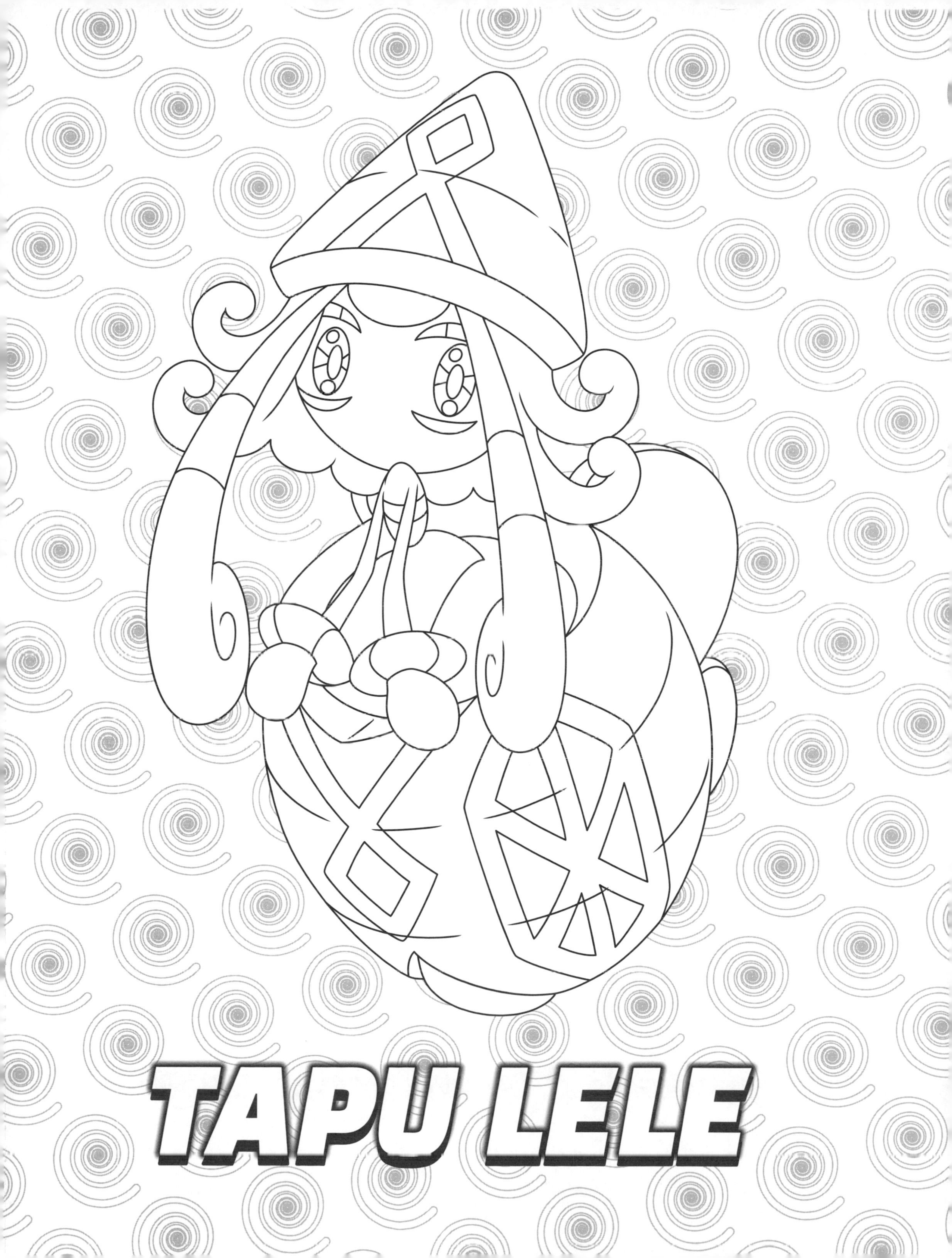
TAPU LELE

ZARUDE